THE
OLD ONES

THE
OLD ONES

Their aim? To get there quick . . .
before something gets them . . .

CREATIVE WRITING PRODUCTIONS

authorHOUSE®

AuthorHouse™
1663 Liberty Drive
Bloomington, IN 47403
www.authorhouse.com
Phone: 1-800-839-8640

Published by AuthorHouse   05/11/2012

ISBN: 978-1-4678-9649-8 (sc)
ISBN: 978-1-4678-9650-4 (e)

Any people depicted in stock imagery provided by Thinkstock are models, and such images are being used for illustrative purposes only.
Certain stock imagery © Thinkstock.

This book is printed on acid-free paper.   .

Because of the dynamic nature of the Internet, any web addresses or links contained in this book may have changed since publication and may no longer be valid. The views expressed in this work are solely those of the author and do not necessarily reflect the views of the publisher, and the publisher hereby disclaims any responsibility for them.

Follow us on Facebook: search for James Bookie

Contents

ACKNOWLEDGEMENTS

This story is the first of a group effort, written by a total of six final hands.

It shows what becomes when passions bind together. Out of the six writers-Sam, Ben, Toby, Nick, Becky, and Philippa, three are known dyslexics. Yet it does not stop them. It does not stop their passion. It does not stop their wild imagination, and fascinating knowledge that pours out on a Thursday night onto a small table, tucked between the English and Maths rooms of a small country high school. Nor does it stop them from dreaming throughout the week, or prevent them sharing startling new knowledge with their co-workers; opening a fascinating new world that many knew little about . . .

For each of us there was a role; Ben and Becky store between them a mine of knowledge on alternate worlds, and the dark and mysterious myths behind them. Sam has the film aspect; what has been seen before, and suggested ideas for when we got truly stuck. Nick was part of the original four-a rock in the after-school writing group. When he left for college, Philippa rejoined, able to now pick up the fascinating new story, now an after school PE club had stopped, and Toby tagged along, aiding and assisting with ideas that were mostly, truly bizarre.

Personally, I would like to thank Miss Clarke, whose great idea it was to begin the writing club. I would like to thank my co-workers and friends for turning up every Thursday, though they may have had better things to do. I would also like to thank my English Teacher, Mr Bish, who taught me not only the powers of language, but the power of imagination, throughout my three lower-school years. Thank you for your inspiration.

Philippa Wheatley.

Writers and Authors from Years 10 and 11:

Samantha Bill (Y11)
Philippa Wheatley (Y11)
Nicholas Vaughan (Y11)

Rebekah Jones (Y10)
Benjamin Watkins (Y10)
Toby Collier (Y10)

The above group would also like to thank our proof reader, Sally Dix. This book is also a dedication to Samantha's mother, Angela, for her kind heart and fighting spirit.

Without you, this book would not be.

Thank you also to contributors of Wikipedia-the free encyclopedia, for their information on Redcaps, Cthulus and Wolfsbane.

Follow us on Facebook: James Bookie
Go online: http://creativewriting090.webs.com
Order online at: www.authorhouse.com

Red Cap

Size: Average
Special Power: Dash
Height: 5 ft. 11 in. (1.80 m)
Weight: 170 lbs. (77 kg)

British folklore has many stories of evil goblins called Redcaps. They live in ruined castles and attack anyone who dares enter.

A Redcap Amulet is the most common and important piece of equipment. A powerful, yet easy-to-control Titan, Redcaps make the perfect first Amulet for devoted operatives.

A Redcap is an intimidating storm of claws and teeth, muscle and bone. His red eyes strike fear into the enemies of the Organization and his presence alone is often enough to break the will of a captive Seeker.

In ancient times, the Egyptian general Dovhi-tep possessed a dozen Redcap Titans himself, and over the course of many years he built up the focus to control them all at once. This army of terrifying Titans led Dovhi-tep to many victories and established his (and Redcap's) reputation as a force to be reckoned with.

Alex's Fear

T HE BLACK HEAVENS opened, unleashing a blood red bolt of lighting over a house. Outside, dark brown roots crept up thin walls. Inside, there was turmoil.

"Get back here!" shouted a step-mother, talking to a young boy, kept in jeans and a hoody, slouching on the stairs.

"Leave me alone. You're not my mum!" the boy shouted back, his face partly covered by his favourite top.

"Don't talk to your mother like that!"
"*She is not my Mum!*"

Alex charged up stairs in a mood. It looked like he couldn't do anything, and he was sick of it. He kicked his door open. Sitting down on his bedroom floor, he noticed a red leather book on the floor. Thoughts clouded his mind, angry and resentful.

Great, they bought me another journal. Fine! They want me to write down my feelings, so now I will!

The boy threw opened the journal and wrote. Six, simple, angry words.

I wish my parents were dead.

What happened next is something Alex couldn't explain until many years later. For, suddenly, the words disappeared, sucked away into an abyss, and another reappeared.

Granted.

What? thought Alex, staring at the words on the page, *What the . . . ?*

"AAAAARRRRHHHH!"

Screams echoed from downstairs. Alex shut the journal. *No! This was crazy!*

"MUM! DAD!" he shouted, leaping through the door, thundering down the steps.

What was going on?! Where were they?!

Panicking, he searched through doorways. It was like there was no-one there.

"Mom, Dad, *where are you?!*"

PUFF! Two, small, gremlin looking creatures appeared as if from nowhere. Tall and muscular, their beady eyes feasted on the floor below. A strange red substance was dripping from their tongues. Alex too, looked at the floor, and instantly felt sick. Beneath them lay two bodies. Two, familiar, lifeless, blood-dripping bodies. His parents.

"Mum? Dad? I take it back! I TAKE IT BACK!" he begged, but there was nothing he could do. The gremlins were fading.

Then, they were gone.

CHARLIE'S FEAR

CHARLIE WALKED INTO the room, slammed the door and slumped across his chair. He felt dazed. The world seemed to swim before him. He put a hand to his sweating forehead, bringing it away to show a shining wet palm. He looked up across the shining room out of the wide-pan windows to the skyscrapers of New York City. What a morning. The beautiful scene lay outstretched before the . . . no, wait. What was that? Something was hurtling towards him. Something at the speed of lightning. Charlie squinted across the sunlit room. What the . . . ? What was it? It was . . . . Oh GOD!

In the split second that he remained conscious, Charlie can remember only two things-a horrid, sinking feeling, and a sudden burning, aching, excruciating pain, more powerful and blinding than anything he had ever felt before. His eyes popped, blood vessels screaming as coloured circles flickered and vanished. A high pitched scream, so loud he thought his skull would shatter. A shriek of glass, a sudden image of a blood-stained man, slumped against a high backed chair . . . and then no more.

He woke to a sickening, burning feeling in his abdomen. His eyes blurred and flashed. His head span. He reeled over to be sick, and placed his hand is something that was astoundingly hot. Snatching his hand away, he realised what his pain sensors were trying to tell him.

Fire. Flames, flames as high as the office ceiling, bearing down on him. He opened his dry mouth to scream, and inhaled a mouthful of smoke. Coughing and blinded, he stood. His head reeled. He was going to collapse.

Got to get out, he thought, blindly, staring around at the burning walls. He turned. There was a gap to his right. He ran through. Flames missed his foot by inches, scorching heat running across the soles. Charlie could feel it in his toes, couldn't tell whether he was on fire or not. His whole body felt numb, sickening, out of control. There was a sudden scream and the sound of a crashing window. He reached the door and pulled it open, heart racing, and there was another sound of breaking glass.

Charlie felt weary, tired, but for some reason his legs pulled him forwards and he had a dim vision of pitching down the stairs. A woman stood on the platform, arms tangled around the banister, head down. He pulled her arm, and she stumbled, falling almost head first. He let go, and ran down the second flight, the third, the forth, his numb brain telling him at each moment that he was leaving good people behind. Something exploded, and he pitched headfirst across the floor, rolling onto his back. Legs jumped over him, high heels ran past. He writhed madly, avoiding the stampede as black work-shoes thundered past his head. Suddenly all was quiet. He rolled back onto his stomach and there was another explosion from above. Charlie remembers a dull thud across his back. And then . . . nothing.

In his dream, he sees himself again as a jet soars towards him, pilot still firmly strapped in, eyes wide with horror. He sees himself again and again, every time the same, every time a nightmare. Going round, and round, and round . . .

SHEA'S FEAR

F LAMES FLICKERED FROM the candles' wicks, held by men in dark grey robes. They followed a tall, shrouded figure up the marble staircase, and entered a room. Seven tablets hung against seven walls. Each of the figures placed themselves, facing forwards, hoods concealing hidden faces, arms out towards a centred black figure. The chanting began.

The man in the centre chanted louder than the others, repeating several words, words that the others weren't saying.

"Azathoth, Dagon, Nyarlathotep, Yig, Shub-Niggurath, Yog-Sohoth, Cthulhu."

Over and over the words sounded. Not words, but names. And as each one was repeated, a blinding light lit the room, and Shea noticed the tablets had begun to engrave themselves. Symbols began to form; lines and curves, with no obvious meaning.

Suddenly, as the last name left the man's lips, his form contorted. He was suddenly growing, getting larger and more ghastly. Several lights entered the room, running seemingly right into him, then ricocheting out, bouncing off each tablet, spinning past the hooded figures as they ducked. The ground shook in protest, the walls cracking under pressure. The figures screamed and fled, leaving the spirit of the man to spread himself through the room, veiling it in darkness.

ANYA'S FEAR

S HE SAW HER eleven-year-old self, watching him, scared. The giant man embraced the tiny girl in huge muscled arms, and Anya gasped in alarm. She'd seen this before. The young child pulled a huge fake smile, her eyes wide as she pretended to be loved, plucking up the courage to tell him.

"Daddy?"

Anya shivered. She remembered when she used to have call him that. 'I'm your Daddy.' he would say. But Anya had always known he wasn't. She couldn't remember her real father, but this certainly wasn't him. This 'Daddy' had waltzed into their lives when she was four, attracted by her mother's vulnerability, and her money. But he wasn't a natural father. She certainly didn't like being left alone with him. In fact, she'd do anything to avoid it, often running off to a friend's house. There was just something in his manner; the way he talked down to her that always made her feel uneasy. It was as if he didn't know how to address her-didn't know how to cope with her growing stronger and smarter, while he just aged. And now . . .

"Daddy, Viktoriya was round here Sunday," she heard herself say, in her fluent Russian tongue. "And we were playing a game. And the pot on the mantle-piece . . . it got broken."

The hug froze. Anya could see the brutish arms tense, her eleven year old self ensnared within them.

"What?"

"It was an accident, Daddy." she heard the child plead, changing it's tone, knowing instantly it had picked the wrong moment. "We were playing and I put my arm out and it broke."

This wasn't strictly true. Viktoriya, good old ten year old Viki, had been distraught at what she'd done, but Anya, brave or foolish, she didn't know, had decided to take the blame. She didn't want her parents angry at her best friend, too. Not Viki.

"What was *Viktoriya* doing round *here?*" she heard the man ask, poison in his voice. It was a tone completely different to that he'd used only minutes ago, when he'd held her tight. It was a tone full of anger, of rage. Of vengeance.

"It was an accident." she heard the child say.

Anya watched, heat rising in her back, as the giant pulled the girl from his grasp and stood up. He was tall, intimidating by anyone's standards. Anger boiled on his face, a rage terrible and true.

"I thought we told you not to bring your clumsy friends round here!" he snarled, while she, the child, stood dumbly, powerless and terrified under his sudden terrible glare. "Don't tell me your mum said we could have her!"

The young girl gaped silently, like a fish out of water, struggling for the words that would protect her mother.

"TELL ME!"

A muscled arm shot out and grasped the child by the hair, wrenching it from her scalp, and she saw the young girl blink and gasp in sudden pain.

"Why was she here? TELL ME!"

"I invited her round!" the child whined, tears welling in her eyes, not daring to pull away from the ferocious grip that held her. The man yanked his arm and, the child fell towards him.

"I told you we couldn't have her round!" he yelled, his grip tight, pulling her head as the child struggled, "Why don't you *listen* to me, HUH?!"

He raised his other hand and Anya turned away, her breathing hot.

"SMACK!"

The noise echoed round the room, as he delivered a blow that sent the child pirouetting to the floor. He reached down and grabbed her by the shoulders, shaking her violently.

"YOU! STUPID! CHILD!" he hissed, each word a bitter harshness to her ears. "You should *NEVER* go running to Mummy! You do as *I* tell you, ALRIGHT?!"

The child nodded dumbly, it's face an inch from his scowling redness, tears streaming down it's cheeks. The man raised another fist, and delivered a second sharp slap, striking the child once again to the ground. Anya knew her cheeks were stinging, a bitter mix of pain and tears. Her own cheeks were burning, and she felt sick.

"We'll see your mother about this!" the man told her, watching the child cower on the ground, it's shoulders shaking as it tried to suppress huge racking sobs. Then he stepped over her, and marched off; ready to find his second victim.

ANYA GETS A CALL

ANYA WALKED INTO the office, and picked up the article. It was a printout-a draft of a yet to be released speech.

> *Teenagers Slain at Castle*
> *23rd March*

> *"Three young teenagers were brutally murdered at Powrie Castle last night. We don't yet know the cause of death but every available police officer is out looking for the culprit or culprits. Our source, however, has told us that the bodies had deep scratches and bites, possibly caused by some sort of animal.*

> *Locals believe that is the work of the 'Red Caps', an old myth that parents tell their children to keep then indoor after dark, but this reporter finds that explanation too far fetched . . ."*

"Karspaskin! Get in here!" boomed the voice of her editor, James Edwards. Anya sighed.

"Yes." she says, in a sweet angelic voice. With her rustic Russian accent, she could get away with most things. Not her boss.

She entered his office, and James turned to her. Today, he was wearing a tight green shirt, partnered by some not particularly flattering trousers. Still young, he could act old enough to be her father sometimes. Not that she needed one.

"Karspaskin, I've got a lead that needs following up and you're just the girl for the job." said James, before she'd even sat down. "It involves travelling to Scotland."

He had that old ring of authority in his voice again, Anya noticed. That was the thing about James. It was the whole thing about England. You could always tell when he was excited. He'd spring up on you like an excitable puppy, ramming information down your throat before you'd even had time to make yourself comfy.

"All the way to Scotland, James?" Anya fished, wondering if this had anything to do with the article she had just picked up. After all, it had been left on *her* desk.

"So? You want the job or not?"

"I don't know. Can I know what your lead is, James?"

Anya felt tired. He always did this, always. He'd let you have just a taste of something, before he leapt on you and demanded to know whether you could do it or not. Mind you, 'no' wasn't really an answer, not as far as he was concerned.

"Sure; you remember that newspaper article, about those kids being murdered by what some locals believed was the so-called 'Red Caps'? There's been another attack, and I think we have a copy-cat killer on the loose. What do ya say Anya, you in or not?"

Anya thought this was all a bit brisk.

"Well, I . . ."

It was time to weigh up her options. So far, they stood like this. One: she didn't really have anything to do in the office. So far she was chasing up the local Peterborough house leads, and comforting though this was in one sense, it was also mighty boring. It didn't surprise her James had chosen her for the job; she was after all, reigning queen when it came to unsolved mysteries. Not that she liked murders, particularly. Still, she could always do with a few more unsolved cases. It might help her get closer to what she was looking for. And maybe, just maybe . . .

"Okay: I'm in." she agreed, resentfully. She couldn't really refuse. She was the undisputed 'paranormal pixie' of the office. Murders and such were her thing, and James wouldn't think twice about sending her off to somewhere like Scotland. He'd just think it was all in a days work.

"Great. Now go home and pack; your train leaves tomorrow at 9:30am."

Anya sighed. Already, a list was forming in her head of what to take. She'd need all the usuals-toothbrush, toothpaste, pyjamas. Hopefully someone would let her borrow a jacket-she didn't know much about Scotland, apart from it was damned cold, and she had no doubt she'd struggle to get all her clothes in. Her boss turned and gave her what he thought was a winning grin, and she rose and left the office.

LIFE UPSIDE DOWN

ALEX WAS BUYING a newspaper. One article grabbed his attention:

PRICELESS ANTIQUE ON OFFER AT LOCAL SHOP.

He read on.

'A jewel incrusted pure gold Aztec dagger has been acquired by local shop owner Morris Finch. Held here by Shea, an employee of the store, the Aztec Dagger is priceless . . . .'

Alex's mind wandered. That was what he had to steal. That's what that stranger had said; the one he had met so long ago. Well, there it was, at last. Nothing to do now but wait. All would be quiet until after dark. It would be a slow day.

It might surprise you, but Alex didn't have a problem with stealing. After all, he had been doing so now for most of his life. Eighteen years was not long, but he had spent a good seven in and out of police stations, or hiding out behind bins, perfecting his technique . . . who wouldn't, if they were like him? If they were . . . *different* . . .

When his parents had died, Alex had been seen as the tragic hero, the little boy lost, tormented with gibberish nonsense about red looking monsters with blood stained teeth-clearly a young boy in distress. And of course, eleven was still young. No wonder the boy's mind had been turned. That's what the police had said. Everyone else just presumed his parents had just had enough of him. Just gone out one day, and left the stupid little half-wit behind. And anyway, *who could have blamed them* . . .

Alex had been shipped from foster home to foster home, but none of them had ever felt like home to him. Perhaps 'home' wasn't the right word, rather more 'loony bin' or 'centre for the dysfunctional'. Or perhaps they should have just called it 'the asylum-a place for those no-one else wants'.

Yes; that's what they had felt like; that horrid word 'asylum'. Keeping him locked in after hours, all day, in case he did *something silly.* But Alex, tired and tormented, had, by nature, frequently learnt the best way to slip out after hours. To begin with he'd got into bad company, drinking and smoking with older boys til they were past drunk. Then, silently, he'd slip off home. But somehow, his 'parents' found out. And when they found out what he *was*, well, it was just too much for them to *even consider* . . .

So he'd turned to crime. It was easy enough. Watch the patterns, the movements. At least Charlie had taken him in. Charlie was, of course, the whole reason he was doing this. Alex had always wondered why he'd done it; there was something about him that just didn't make sense. For one his New York twang. Alex had asked him if he was American. *Yes*, had come the reply, *I used to live there.* But beyond that there was no explanation.

That night, Alex was drawn towards Finchley's, just before closing time. Inside the shop, all was quiet.

It wasn't hard to find. Instantly he found his way to the counter, and picked up the dagger; not too hard-the assistant hadn't been watching it. It was just left on the side, presumably while she attended another customer, and seemed to have forgotten all about it. He held it up, a smile spreading across his narrow lips. It was so easy!

But slipping the dagger in his black leather jacket, Alex noticed he'd begun to feel strange. The feeling came upon him within seconds-like a tingling, spreading from the tips of his fingers all down his back. Feeling as though he was being watched, Alex slowly turned around. Hanging on a long silver chain against the opposite wall was a wolf, hanging silver on it's chain. Its red eyes burned in his face, and he was strangely drawn to it. He stretched out a hand, wanting to take it, to hold it. Cold flesh touch metal, and he reeled back in pain. Up came his palm. Deep in the flesh burnt a mark, black and singeing against his copper skin. A wolf. The talisman had been blessed.

His actions had attracted attention. The kindly assistant approached him.

"Are you okay? What happened?" she asked.

"Nothing. I'm fine." Alex lied. The girl turned, and he made a dash for the door.

Something gleaming her eye. As Shea looked back, she saw at once the dagger was missing. So was the boy. She dashed to the window, but it was too late. Both had gone.

He *must* have taken it. It was strange; Shea couldn't believe she had just seen someone steal. He must have stolen it; there was no-one else there, apart from her. Who else could it have been? And, what was more, how on earth was she going to explain to Mr Finch what had happened? The jewel was priceless; he had told her to take good care of it only that morning. She wished she had never taken it out of the case. It was the most prized piece in the shop; normally they never sold much, just a few bits to odd people passing through. And they were odd people. Some *were* normal, well, normalish, but the odd few passing through Fort Augustus were just downright strange. Occasionally they had an outright wacko off the street come in to steal something or take a bit of a lark. It wasn't an expensive shop, and thieves often went out as empty handed as they had come in. But this, this was bad. Bad with a capital B. She had failed her duty-a very simple duty-of simply looking after the shop. Sell stuff you have, order things you don't. It wasn't too difficult. And above all, don't let thieves in.

Shea sighed. She supposed she would have to ring the police. She went to the back room, found the none-emergency number and dialled. A gruff sounding man answered.

"Hello? This is Police Constable Fletchley. Can I help?"

Shea wearily explained her predicament with the weird looking boy. The Constable took the details, and told her he'd be round at ten 'o' clock tomorrow. Then there really was no more to do. Tired and miserable, Shea closed the shop, and went home.

Anya Leaves Town

A NYA WAS ON the platform, waiting for the train that would take her onwards and upwards to the dreary drizzling country that lay north of her beloved England. The news on the station screen replayed that which she had seen earlier. She sighed; it still gave her no lead. Not that she expected it to; that was the reason she was being sent away, after all; to 'find the facts'. She hoped she could. Sitting in a nice warm office, pursuing an article about werewolves or vampires, might have been easier than travelling to a drizzly cold country to find out murder facts. Still, she was a journalist, and to get the best results, she knew she had to get out in the field. She'd just prefer a field that was not so knee high in highland muck, that was all.

The brakes of a train squealed as it slowed towards the bustling platform. She boarded, knowing it would be dark before she stepped off again, the doors closing firmly behind her with a swish. She found a seat and, stowing her bag firmly in the compartment above, sat there. She was going to be there a long time.

Outside, the noise gathered as the carriage hummed on its wires, waiting. From the platform a guard whistled, and waved. The vibration started, as slowly beneath, the wheels began to turn, gathering momentum as they span faster, and faster. With a final hiss, the train screeched out of the darkening station, onwards towards the unknown.

An Interesting Meeting

ABOUT 9PM, THE pub was crowded and smoky. Alex entered and looked around. He struggled to the bar and ordered a drink. A couple of minutes passed. He felt edgy, nervous, more aware of the valuable item about his person. Sipping his beer, he sat, watching the door intently. More minutes passed. He could not wait forever; he wanted this over and done with, but so far no-one had shown. He looked around at the crowded backdrop: men were lost in conversation, tucked into the safety of their own little world. Half an hour passed, and still no-one was here. Alex finished his glass. It was a bum deal. He'd just missed out on big stakes. He would have to leave; sell it to someone else. He turned for the door, and a dark figure watched him, sat in a small alcove. It blew out cigarette smoke and slowly nodded it's head. Glancing across, Alex saw. It was him.

As he approached, Alex tried to guess the age of the man. If it was a man. He couldn't see all of the face, only his lips and dark chin; more the physique that gave it away. Alex thought it odd the buyer should have his hood up. Normally the buyer was an older collector, like those he had sold to in the past. The man finished his cigarette and motioned for Alex to sit down. Willing his legs to move forward, Alex slid onto the stool opposite. He had a sudden strange feeling he was in over his head; not something that normally happened. Really, what was he thinking? He was used to this! Cold shivers ran down his spine. He waited.

"You got it?" the stranger rasped, in a surprisingly choked voice that Alex would have associated more with a long-time smoker.

"Depends. You got money?"

"Yes. Show me!"

Cautiously Alex opened his jacket revealing the left inside pocket. Careful not to let anyone but the man opposite see, he slowly lifted the cloth, the handle of the dagger just peeking over the top of the pocket. He wrapped the cloth back over and closed his coat. The man gave a smile and nodded.

"Take your jacket off, leave it on the table."

"Why?"

"Don't ask me why, just do it!"

Alex looked questioningly as he removed his jacket.

"There is another jacket on the back of your chair. Put it on, in the inside pocket is what you came for."

Alex put on the jacket, immediately feeling the difference in weight to his own and quickly stole a look at the cash.

"It's all in there, don't bother counting it!"

'This isn't how I usually do business." said Alex.

The stranger sat. Alex couldn't tell if he was breathing or not. It was like sitting with a statue. The whole cloak was still. The stranger spoke again.

"Out of interest, where did you acquire such an item?" he rasped, in his deep, cancerous voice.

"You'll know soon enough." Alex said, simply. He didn't like the man. Shivers were still running down his back, and the hair on the back of his neck was on end. Still: rule number one: don't tell the buyer how to acquire. Charlie had taught him that. Do that, and you'd lose your whole business; something which, in their current state, neither of them could afford. Still, tonight it felt like he'd just hit the jackpot.

Having got what he wanted, and wanting nothing more to do with the strange, cloaked man, Alex rose, and headed directly towards the door, trying to shake the creeping feeling that he was being watched. He left the bar, leaving the stranger behind in a swirl of cigarette smoke, smiling with blood red lips.

THEFT ON THE NEWS

THE POLICE WERE being particularly unhelpful.

So far, all they had managed to establish was that, yes, indeed, somebody had stolen the valuable item, but for some strange reason, not one of the detectives had managed to lift a single fingerprint from the scene, including the wolf talisman.

No-one had come near the shop all day. Police frightened people, even the locals. Mr Finch was tottering around, looking more and more unstable. Shea felt sorry for him; he had probably spent most of his life in the shop, and the dagger had been one of the most expensive possessions he'd ever held. From the other side of the room, one of the constables came to her.

"Have you found anything?" asked Shea.

"Not yet."

Shea sighed. They were absolutely useless.

"It's a case most strange," said the Constable, quoting Poirot "Are you sure he touched the necklace?"

"Yes. He must have. He got burnt."

The policeman offered her a look. "Right. Well we can't lift anything from it. Are you sure you don't know where he went?"

Shea sighed.

"I'd have told you if I knew." she told him, impatiently. "I've never seen him before. He might live around here, but then I wouldn't know."

"Well," said the Constable "then I think we've done all we can do today."

Shea looked round. There were about five officers probing and shining torches in the most inconspicuous of places.

"Fine." she said "What do you want me to do? Am I alright to open up? It's just that we're a single shop. We're losing our income. People might start to talk."

"Yes, that's fine. People will be interested anyway. I was talking to a young woman this morning. She was asking about the deaths at Fort Augustus. Y'know-those two lads?"

"Yeah," Shea responded, nonchalantly "What happened to them?"

"Well, we're not sure. It seems to be leading us nowhere."

"Hang on!" Shea failed to grasp the concept. "Two lads, murdered, and you don't know how they died?"

"Oh, we know how all right. Bled to death, it would seem. But by who? That's the question."

Yes, thought Shea. That *is* the question. One *you* should be answering.

"Anyway, the girl's a news reporter. There might just be something to it. Y'know, put out a statement. People might recognise this lad."

"Right." said Shea, "Thanks very much for your help. I'll get onto it. Do you know where I can get her?"

"I'll set it up for you."

Normally, Shea would have resisted. She didn't like some of the lies in the newspapers-often she thought the whole thing was a waste of a tree-but seeing as the entire police force had failed to do anything useful today, she agreed.

"Okay," she said "just let me know. You've already got the number. Just tell me when it's all set up."

Two days later, Shea received a phone call. It was the Constable.

"Hello, this is Finchley's. Can I help you?"

"Hello; it's Constable Fletchley. Just to let you know the young girl will meet you in the library tomorrow, at half two."

"Thank you Constable."

"No problem."

ANYA GETS A LEAD

"KARSPASKIN? IT'S JAMES, your editor."

Anya sighed. It was the day after the journey. The long ride had taken hours, to the point where Anya thought she'd probably spend pretty much the rest of her life on the train. They had passed from London's Kings Cross, through Peterborough, Grantham, Newmark North Gate, Doncaster, York, Darlington, Durham, Newcastle, Alnmouth, Berwick-upon-Tweed, Dunbar, Edinburgh Waverly, and Haymarket, to Dundee. It had taken her nearly eleven hours. By the time she arrived in the busy station it was nearly 7am the next day. Then of course, she had to swap to the more local trains, through Perth, and Inverness, to Helmsdale, taking yet another seven hours. By the time she had arrived at around three 'o' clock, Anya was pleased to get off. Having slept onboard, she was not as tired as she thought she would be. Still, she booked herself into the nearest hotel, fell on the bed and slept. Now she was awake, Anya had freshened up, only to find a whole series of unanswered calls on her phone from her editor. Reluctantly, she had listened in. Yep, there he was, barking out instructions to her, in an excited, electronic voice.

"Anya, turn on the TV. There's some really great news. It might be a lead for you."

Wearily, Anya found the remote and flicked it on. Sky News was showing a woman dressed in red. She seemed to be on a high street-there were cars in the background, standing outside an ordinary little shop. Anya managed to hook on.

". . . on Wednesday when it was stolen from this shop. Mr Finch, what does this mean to you?"

A wizened, stooped little man in corduroy trousers appeared. He looked at least sixty.

"Well, a' mean, it's a terrible blow." he was saying, in a wheezy voice that Anya was surprised he could even muster, "This dagger's the most important theng we've go' in this shop. 'S a valuable artefact. Y'carn jus' go nickin' this thengs; is just no' right."

The woman turned back to the screen.

"This is Amanda Bullock, reporting for Sky News. Back to you, Chris."

Anya decided to go out. It was early morning, and she felt like she'd just lost the last two days to a fuzz of travelling. She breezed around, hoping to find somewhere nice to eat. Her phone rang again.
"Hello?"
"Hi, Anya, it's James. Did you get the news?"
"Well, not really. It was coming to the end of the report by the time I'd tuned in."

James started talking, and Anya zoned out. From his babbling he seemed to be telling her that the shop broken into was holding a very ancient Aztec Dagger, worth possibly millions. Anya wondered vaguely how on earth it had managed to find its way to such a scutty little place.

". . . so they phoned down *here*, and the Met were looking for you. They wanted to know if you knew anything about it?"

Anya woke up.

"Hmmm?"

She heard James sigh.

"About the dagger, Anya. Do you know anything about it?"

"Not really, no."

James sighed again.

"Well . . . there's a woman up there who was in the shop at the time. It's something to report, isn't it? Not ghouls, exactly, or the mad underworld, but it's something."

"Mmmm."

"I've told her you'll meet her in the Helmsdale Library at two thirty tomorrow. Got it?"

"Yep."

"You are there, aren't you?"

"Yep."

"Good. Well, call me soon, then. Bye!"

ANYA MEETS SHEA

A NYA HAD NO idea where the lead would take her.

So far, all she had seen of Scotland, was not the magnificent mountains, or wild culture, but a rather crowded little town in which she was now a temporary resident, sited at the Moonlit Palisade, which looked anything but. Still, she had been told to meet her there, this woman, at the library, two-thirty. Anya looked at her watch. Two 'o' clock glowed in luminescent green. She still had time to kill.

She took another turn up the high-street. Shopping, thought Anya, always made her feel happy, despite the only things in the windows being badly made tartan patterns, aimed at inexperienced tourists, and could hear traffic from the busy street. Men were telling jokes and laughing, children playing in the warm sunshine. She smiled. Her thoughts entered the busy street and wandered.

One day I'd rather like to have children.

Lost in her own world, a sudden knock to the head startled her. A football bounced on the pavement beside. Dimly, Anya looked about for the culprit. A tall man, dressed in a vest and shorts, waved at her. It would have looked nice, except his bulging beer-belly meant it was not befitting of his figure. He apologised, and Anya assured him she was alright, but inside her head was pounding. She walked on, and thought again about having children, trying to alleviate the pain. Inside a conversation was forming.

What's the rush? A voice in her mind said, soothing her, *What's it all for?*

Anya had never really had a boyfriend, not even in Russia. And if James was the best London could do, then she could wait. Anyway, what did she need a boyfriend for? Boys were a pain in the bum; they were a nuisance, always making stupid jokes or wandering round in their macho way. All she needed she already had. She had her senses, she wasn't ill, and she had a good job. She stopped and sniffed, trying to take in something pleasant from her environment, smelling grass, aftershave, perfume . . . and a slight scent of B.O.

At the end of the street, Anya's eye a shop caught her eye. The sign stood in faded yellow italics above a not particularly beguiling door. *Finchleys.* Deciding to look in, to see what was sold there, she peered through the window, noticing all sorts of bizarre things: things that she'd never come across in the highstreets of London: spell books, candles, magic books, talismans, copies of myths, monsters and demon books. The walls were gray and it seemed quite dark inside, erring, even for Anya, towards creepy. Maybe later she might come back, and buy the guys at work something. The girls would love a candle, and she knew one of them who would absolutely love a book on myths, monsters and demons. Anya lifted her nose from the grimy shop window and continued on her way.

At two twenty she headed towards the town library. It was a tall, masterful looking building, as though you'd have to be very intellectual even to walk up the steps. Inside, it was pretty much the same as every library she'd ever come across-quiet as the grave, and packed fit to burst with paper. A woman, dressed in a long overcoat waved at her. She had long, brown hair and a mature expression. Well, that must be her: I mean, no-one else would wave to her in a quiet library, would they? Carefully and slowly, Anya walked over to introduce herself.

The woman's name was Shea, and it was indeed her, who had been sent to meet up with a journalist. The cordial introduction was quickly over, and they sat down at one of the empty tables, shuttered between the bookshelves. Keeping one eye on bustling librarian tottering past on her flimsy high-heels every now and then, Anya began asking all the usual questions, keeping her voice down, trying to build a description of that night. From what she was getting, it seemed pretty ordinary-a shop robbed by a bored adolescent. Run of the mill, really.

"Something strange, I noticed though." said Shea, after describing what had gone on. "There was this wolfs talisman left on the desk, like in the shape of a wolf. It was red hot."

Anya looked up at her.

"Hot?"

"Yes," Shea replied, looking equally baffled. "It was red hot to the touch, you know? Like it was burning or something."

Anya smiled. Now, that *was* interesting. She knew what *that* meant. She was, after all, the expert on such things. Perhaps this lead was turning out to be more than it had originally appeared. She probed.

"Tell me, was it made of wolfs bane?"

Shea stared blankly at her.

"What?"

"Wolfs bane. It's like a magic ingredient."
Shea shrugged.
"I dunno. Probably. Shop's got all sorts of weird stuff in. It was a wolf talisman."
"What was it used for?"
"Err . . . keeping away wolves?"

Anya reached into her bag, pulled out her book, and read quietly, keeping her voice down.

> *'Aconitum, pronounced A-co-ní-tum, known as aconite, monkshood, wolfsbane, leopard's bane, women's bane, Devil's helmet or blue rocket is a genus of flowering plant belonging to the buttercup family. There are over 250 species of Aconitum.*
> *The most common plant in this genus, Aconitum napellus (the Common Monkshood) was considered in the past to be of therapeutic and toxicological importance. Its roots have occasionally been mistaken for horseradish. When touched to one's lip, the juice of the aconite root produces a feeling of numbness and tingling. This plant is used as a food plant by some Lepidoptera species including Dot Moth, The Engrailed, Mouse Moth, Wormwood Pug, and Yellow-tail, but it is toxic to many other species. Upon ingestion, marked symptoms may appear almost immediately, usually not later than one hour, and with large doses death is almost instantaneous. Death usually occurs within 2 to 6 hours in fatal poisoning. The initial signs are gastrointestinal including nausea, vomiting, and diarrhoea, followed by a sensation of burning, tingling, and numbness in the mouth and face, and of burning*

in the abdomen. In severe poisonings pronounced weakness occurs and sensations of tingling and numbness spread to the limbs. Other features may include sweating, dizziness, difficulty in breathing, headache, and confusion. Cardiovascular features include hypotension, bradycardia, sinus tachycardia, and ventricular arrhythmias. Causes of death are paralysis of the heart or of the respiratory centre. The only post-mortem signs are those of asphyxia, or suffocation.'

"Handy." said Shea, as she looked up. "But how does it keep away wolves?"

"Well, wolves have to ingest it." Anya replied, carefully "I suppose if they swallowed the talisman, it would kill them."

"But wouldn't the person wearing it be dead?"

"Well, yes, if the wolves got them. But it's not just wolves people fear. After all, there aren't many wolves roaming round Scotland. Least not that I've seen."

"So what's it for?"

"Well, according to this book, wolfs bane is a toxin to those who are half-blood."

"Half blood?"

"Yeah, like non-human."

The woman opposite stared blankly at her. Anya sighed. "*Werewolves.*" she said, pointedly.

Shea's face did not change. She only looked disbelieving.
"Werewolves?"

"Yep."

"But-werewolves. Like . . . the legend?"

"Not a legend." Anya told her. "It's a fact."

"Like in *Children of the Vampire*."

"Right."

"You don't seem to believe me."

Shea shrugged "Well, it's not very believable, is it?"

Anya handed her the book. "Here." she said "Read."

> *'Wolfsbane has been ascribed with supernatural powers in the mythology relating to werewolves and other lycanthropes, either to repel them, relating to aconite's use in poisoning wolves and other animals, or in some way induce their condition, as aconite was often an important ingredient in witches' magic ointments. In folklore, aconite was also said to make a person into a werewolf if it is worn, smelled, or eaten. They are also said to kill werewolves if they wear, smell, or eat aconite. Other accounts claim wolfsbane is used as a brew to prolong the condition in the event a werewolf became under the full moon's influence.'*

"So it might keep them alive?"

"Not by what you're telling me. Sounds like this someone got burnt. Put it with those strange deaths you keep having, and there might be a link."

Shea folded her arms. "I don't see it." she said.

"I do." Anya replied, getting to her feet. "Trust me. Thanks for the number. I'll be in touch."

FINDING THE
CULPRIT

"**A**RE YOU SURE this is it?"

Shea stood outside the great oak door. The two girls stood at the edge of the forest, enshadowed by a hulking figure of a run-down shack, seemingly made from poor quality wood. The windows were smeared and grimed, as though from centuries of neglect and hardship. The brick that could be seen had paled, as if the dust settled upon it had merged into one, and tiles appeared to be falling from the roof.

Anya nodded. "That's it."

Shea stared back at the door. It was over a week since Anya had first been in touch, and this is where it had led them; to a stranger's door just outside the edge of the forest. It had taken them almost three hours of driving to get there. The door must have been six foot high, and looked impenetrable as stone. There was no knocker. Feeling intimidated, but determined, none-the-less, Shea lifted one gloved hand, and proceeded to knock three times on the great oak door.

They waited in silence, as the many rooks cawed down from the great pine trees, but no-one answered. Shea stepped across the beaten brickwork, and peered in through the lace-lined window. Past the grease lay a simple room; one table, a bed, a few cupboards and what appeared to be a huge pink armchair next to an open fire. She squinted, trying to determine light from the grate, but her perception was fogged by the dirty windows, and she couldn't see. Stepping back in frustration, she realised that no smoke came from the chimney stack, sitting high on its deformed base, cracked and unsightly. She was determined to be patient. If anyone lived here, they weren't likely to escape *her*. No, she would simply wait. If no-one was in, well, she could sit here all day for all she cared. That knife was of great importance to her; after all, it was her fault it had been taken in the first place. It was the most expensive thing they'd owned. The weapon had to be found.

Shea knocked again on the dry wood, and promptly sat down on the dusty brick step. The material seemed dry and brittle, cracked and yet resolute, as if it too, had been here a long time, waiting to be let in. Shea folded her thin arms across her chest, and waited.

It was ten whole minutes before the door opened. Then, a sudden click; the great unmoving sound of heavy wood, as it was drawn back. Shea stood, and found herself face to face with . . . a boy. Or rather, he looked like a boy from the outside. Shea stared. No, he couldn't be-not out here on his own. She peered at him closely. Now she looked she'd put her more in his early twenties. A clean, shaven, thickset face and dark brown eyes stared back at him. The boy seemed to be wearing almost combat-style clothes; a black t-shirt with thickset trousers and high-laced mountain boots. He clearly hadn't been expecting them, for he stared incomprehensively at her, surprise showing in his slack face and widened deep-set eyes.

Shea stared at him. By God; this journalist was a mind-reader. From a simple sketch she had sent later that day, the woman had led her right to her intruder's front door. The resemblance was uncanny. She was in no doubt it was him.

"Hello." Anya introduced herself, getting ahead while Shea took in his palid features. "I'm Anya, I'm a journalist, and I'm working on a local case you might have heard about a few days ago, when an exceedingly rare and expensive knife was taken from Finchley's Magical Store, on the high street? I want to talk to you."

The boy's reaction is slow. He looked up, and stared at her.

"We think," stated Shea, coming quickly to the point, "You took something of mine, and we're here to get it back."

The boy stared blankly at them. Shea sighed, dropped her brown backpack off her shoulders, and rummaged inside.

"This," she cried, holding up a photo of the dagger, "is what you stole, isn't it? We've come to talk to you about it. Now, are you going to let us in, or not?"

Bewildered, the boy stood back from the door, and allowed them inside. The room, though basic, seemed rather tidier than its exterior. No dust had collected on the unvarnished wooden floor. Shea wondered how anyone could live like this, in the untamed, unhomely grotto.

"Where shall we sit?" Shea asked, pointedly. She could not believe she was here, demanding to be sat in a thief's living room. It was unlike anything she'd done before. Yet it had to be him. He had nearly cost her her job. She cared about her work, and she cared for her employer. She was not going without answers.

The boy pointed to a small wooden table that seemed to fit in with the rest of the settings. Shea sat herself down in one of the four wood-backed chairs.

"Right. You are Alex, I think?"

He nodded, almost at the same time Anya, stood behind his back did.

"And you stole this dagger. We've come to reclaim it. If you hand it over, there'll be no trouble, but if you don't, we'll be forced to call the police. It doesn't seem like you've got yourself a very good record at the moment, so a bit of co-operation wouldn't go amiss. Now, where is it?"

The boy stared blankly at her. He appeared almost bored, listless, lifeless.

"Haven't got it."

"Now listen here," started Shea, "I've asked you nicely and all you have to do is co-operate. I've told you, you won't be in any trouble, but you see the thing is, this dagger is of rather greater significance than you probably think. Now-"

"I haven't got it."

"What do you mean? Of course you've got it; you stole it from her shop weeks ago."

"No, I haven't. I gave it to someone."

"You *gave it* to someone?" Shea asked in disbelief "And who might this someone be?"

Alex shrugged.

"Nobody."

"Listen," instructed Shea, eager to get matters rolling. "You *do* know, I know you do. Just tell me. Who was it? A colleague, or a friend, who?"

Alex shrugged again. "No-one."

"Listen," Shea tried "I've got information on you, and if you don't tell me where the dagger is, I'll release it to the press, then everyone will know who you are! Anya here is a journalist, isn't that right, Anya?"—Anya nodded—"Now just tell me and the whole thing will be dropped!"

The boy seemed to squirm before her. At the sound of "I've got information on you" the boy's eyes had widened suddenly and he had seemed more alert in his chair. When she had reached "Everyone will know who you are!" Shea knew she definitely held his attention. She was not afraid to expose him for the thief and coward that he was. His demeanour had changed completely. He seemed wide-eyed and alert.

Internally Alex was panicking. This woman knew all about him. She knew all about his . . . ways . . . and now she was threatening to release the whole of it to the press! Surely no-one would believe her. She wouldn't really tell everyone he was a . . . well, y'know . . . on the other hand, Charlie was his best mate, *and* his employer, and he didn't want him to be caught. Privately and hurriedly weighing up the possibilities, Alex decided neither was a particularly good choice. However, things at work had been getting stranger. Charlie had recently landed him in several sticky situations, not omitting the recent and most strange scenario in the pub, when the man he had dealt with had completely refused to show his face. Yes, things were getting odd, and as the underhand of the gang, Alex wasn't going to take the blame. Charlie could surely get himself out of this bizarre fix. He, Alex, had only done what he had been asked him to do, and had been caught. Still, if they were both caught . . . who would get him out then? Alex didn't much like the thought of prison. There was no room for werewolves there.

"We won't get your friend into trouble." crooned Shea, as if she had been reading his every thought.

Alex frowned. Well, so much for the long shot. Charlie could explain; he was the one getting the most pay, anyhow. He was the one in charge.

"Okay." he agreed, accepting their offer, "I'll take you."

THE FAMOUS FOUR

TWO WILLING VOLUNTEERS, and a not so willing confederate, were sitting in the open bar area of Lock Inn, Fort Augustus. It was a 19th Century inn, formerly a bank and post office, sitting at the bottom of the flight of locks on the Caledonian Canal, linking to Loch Oich. Outside the tables overlooked the lock and nearby boats, hired for the day, steamed along the calm waters. It seemed a tranquil spot.

Not for long.

A man entered the bar by a side door, and sat down on one of the red pin cushioned stools. He leant casually across the bar, and muttered something to the barman, who instantly set about making the order. Charlie looked around to the window, and was pleased to se the sun blazing outside, touching the grass, painting it green. Everything so far had gone well. Alex would soon give him the weapon. He supposed the boy must have fallen asleep, and therefore never showed, but that was by-the-by. Any time soon he, Charlie, would be a very rich man.

The barman served him a large beer in a cool glass, and he kissed it gratefully with parched lips. Guinness Extra Stout—an opaque red-brown colour with a creamy, tawny head; very full-bodied, dense and thick, a complex spicy Worcestershire sauce aroma, dry coffee-toffee flavour with a chocolate finish. Delicious in every sense. All he had to do now was wait for

Alex to get the dagger to him; the dagger that would make him deliciously rich.

Across the room, a nervous looking Alex waited. The man turned, showing a pointed, aqua line nose, and cheerful rustic features. That was him.

Across the table, Shea and Anya stared enquiringly at him. Reluctantly, Alex nodded.

The girls took no time to waste as they swept off their seats, and marched up to the bar. Alex cringed. Why had he agreed to this? Both of them would surely get into alot of trouble, and, if they didn't, there was no way Charlie was ever going to let him work for him again. Why oh why?

"Hello." he heard Shea call, "I'm Shea: work for Finchley's in Helmsdale. I'm afraid we have some questions for you."

The look Shea received was as blank as the one she got from Alex when they had accosted him at his home. No wonder they were friends.

"We think," Anya began, working as part of a two-man team, "you have a dagger; a dagger that belongs to Shea, and we want it back."

Charlie stared. Who the hell were these women, and how in God's dear name did they know about the dagger?

"Err . . . what?" he asked.

Anya frowned. There was something definitely not British about him; despite the rustic country-loving coat and hat, she thought she'd heard him speak *American*.

Shea rolled her eyes. "Don't play dumb with me. I know you have it."

Charlie turned balefully, and noticed Alex behind them, who shrugged. Obviously someone had landed themselves a bit of trouble. And he'd brought them to Charlie to sort out.

"They wanted to know where the dagger is," Alex told his employer, and friend. "I told them, I'd sold it."

Charlie choked on his beer, his previous moment's visions of golden bars and clouds, bursting like bubbles.

"You did?!"

There was definitely something in the accent now, Shea noted. She guessed New Yorker.

"Yeah. That's what you wanted, right?"
Charlie stared at Alex. The boy, sweet though he was, and a damned good friend and accomplice, had no idea about money. The dagger was worth million. *Millions.* And he had *sold it?!*
"Well, yeah." said Alex "To that man, y'know?"
"*That man?*"
"Er, excuse me?" said Shea interrupting "Hello? That means you did have it. So that means you haven't got it. So that means you owe us an Aztec dagger worth hundreds."

Charlie could have cried. Hundreds? She had no idea. He turned back to the woman. She had a mature edge to her, but Charlie sensed he could really get her back up if he wanted to.

"Well, ladies, we haven't got it." he said, with an air of forced calm. He turned back to his drink. Half of it had slopped over the bar in his surprise, making a pool on the dark oak surface.

"Do you know," Anya asked, sitting down to Charlie's right, making him feel uncomfortable, "*what* is so valuable about that dagger which you, incidentally, don't have?"

"Yeah," said Charlie, dismayed "the stones. Aztec, aren't they? Should be in a museum. Worth a dollar. Or a thousand. Would have been, if King Kong there-I can't believe you sold it! I told you to sell it *here*, Tuesday!"

"Yeah!" cried Alex, hostile, "I did! On Tuesday, there was a man in here, and we did business. What's the problem?!"

Anya shut her eyes and tried to remain calm. The man was an idiot. How could someone be so foolish as to sell the thing? Charlie, confused, thought the woman was meditating. He went back to his beer.

"No." she said, trying to bring the somewhat meandering conversation back round, "Not the stones, though they are worth a penny. No, what makes that dagger so valuable is what it does-"

"What, slice things?" said Charlie. "Come on. I could have made millions!"

"Not slice things!" Anya hissed. She reached into her holdall and drew out her book, flicking it over to a middle page. In the middle was a drawing, an exact replica of the dagger.

"Nice." said Charlie, giving it a disinterested glance, trying to drown his loss.

"Yes. This is an exact picture of the dagger. Exact. Now, this is a very old piece of metal. It was crafted by Hephaestus, the Greek god of volcanoes, a craftsman and blacksmith. He lusted after Athena, another crafts person. He was thrown from Mt. Olympus and landed in Lemnos where he built his furnaces under a volcano."

Charlie, gaping, thought the two strangers had lost the plot. These women obviously knew something about the dagger. But they were nuts, too.

"Hang on. Hello? Greek gods?" he asked.

"Yes."

"Well, do *you* know where it is?"

"No."

There was an uncomfortable pause.

"Well, then it doesn't matter anyway. We don't have it."

Charlie cut a disdainful look across at Alex, who ducked his head, not wishing to meet his friend's eye.

"Yes," Anya replied. "But that's the thing. You saw it last."

"What? I didn't."

"I wasn't talking about you! You obviously have no idea. You didn't see it last." Shea pointed at Alex "But he did, didn't you?"

Anya turned to another page in her book. It was an old book, with dimmed pages. She stopped. The page held a particularly well-drawn image of a not very handsome man. Actually, Charlie would have gone the full length of saying that this image seemed to be particularly *un*handsome. The man wore a deep black cloak, shrouding most of his body, like he had wrapped it around him from fear of cold. His head was bald; shaved entirely, but Charlie could see the artist had drawn two horn-looking implants on the top. As for his eyes: they were like caves: black and disgustingly acute. Worse of all though was his skin. His face was red; not just blushing red, but full-blown allergic reaction type red, a disgusting elongated black tattoo drawn right over it, in the image of a sun. Charlie wrinkled his nose.

"This is Mr X." Anya told them.

Charlie rolled his eyes. These two women were crazy. He sometimes thought he came up worse for wear in a bar, but . . .

"You have got to be joking." he told them, "Ladies, I know you want the dagger. Neither Alex nor I have got it. So please, leave us alone."

"Mr X is head of the Underworld." Anya continued, ignoring him completely. "He too, comes from the gods. Some say he's Hades, but it's not proven. God of the Underworld and Hell." she added, seeing the boys' blank faces.

"Yeah. So?"

"Well, this Mr X has been in and out all through history. Have you ever heard of the disappearances in the Bermuda? Some say they're down to him. All over Britain, well all over the world, there are gaps, where you can literally step from one place to another-from our world into Hell. They're called portals. They're hidden away. Ever so often, one is discovered. Some last ages, but some just fritter away; it depends on the energy. Anyway, the thing is, this dagger that you've lost, actually opens portals. Now, there's been evidence for some time now that Mr X is actually in our world. We think, though its not yet proven, he's creating an army. There are Redcaps everywhere. That's what we think the deaths were due to-you know, the recent ones in the papers? The lads up at Castle Powrie, and some of the Yorkshire ones too."

Alex had stopped at the word 'Redcaps'. He wrinkled his nose.

"Redcaps?"

Anya flicked to yet another page in her book and showed him a picture. A short, demonic, well built stature stood, brandishing what looked like an angry fist. Around it's waist was a belt make from what appeared to be rats skulls, holding up a weathered loincloth. It's face was covered by a what seemed to be a human skull, it's red eyes gleaming out. On the opposite page was one whose face was uncovered. It looked like Hell; jagged teeth jutting out from it's thick, green lips, stretched in an evil smile.

"But I've seen those!" Alex exclaimed.

Charlie turned and stared down at him. Madness was obviously today's theme.

"Yeah!" Alex exclaimed. "Yeah, I've seen them! They're the ones that killed my Mum and Dad! Y'know: I showed you the papers! Everyone thought I was nuts. Even I thought I was nuts at times. But they're there! I can't believe it! It's definitely them!"

Charlie stared blankly at him, but Anya's eyes narrowed.

"Then," she said, putting two and two together, "Then . . . *yes* . . ."

"Yes, what?"

"*Yes* . . . . I know who you are. Yes, I know *what* you are. That's why you were able to get out of Finchley's before Shea here could see you. Your speed, your obvious strength. Well, it would make sense . . ."

"What would make sense?" asked Alex. He had a sudden very bad feeling. This woman was smart, obviously.

"You're a-"

"SHHH!"

Charlie suddenly broke the conversation. His eyes darted rapidly between them as heads turned, warning them to keep quiet. Anya saw his eyes and knew she'd almost overstepped the mark. This man obviously knew too: they were in this together, she was sure of it. Charlie smiled at the customers, who turned disgruntled back to their food, and Charlie lowered his voice.

"Can we not take this elsewhere?" he hissed.

Shea shook her head and glowered back.

"No. You took something of mine!" she hissed, quietly, aware of the curious diners, "We are not finished!"

Anya was busy shaking her head. That would explain everything. She glanced down at his hand. Yes, there it was: a raw indent in the shape of a wolf talisman.

"You got burnt." she told him, quietly, pointing.

Alex stared down at his hand, then rubbed the other over it, as if to wash it away.

"S'just a mark."

"No," said Anya "It's not. You got burnt by the wolfs bane in that talisman, didn't you?"

Alex shook his head guiltily, and Anya nodded.

"Yeah you did. It just proves everything I-" she glanced around "that I *nearly* said. It's true, isn't it? You are, aren't you?"

Alex didn't answer, but Anya didn't need him to. She'd tell Shea afterwards. It was most interesting. She wondered what it was like to be one; to become a beast once every month. To wake up not knowing where you'd been or who now might be missing. She shuddered at the thrill.

"Anyway," Charlie was saying to Shea, who seemed to still be bickering the same line. "This guy doesn't exist! What proof have you got? A drawing? So you know what Alex is, but this guy, this *guy*, just *isn't* real!"

"Oh surely you can't have missed *all* the strange phenomena going on in the world?!" cried Anya, snapping back in, "Guy de Maupassant's short story, published 1887, about animals that try to posses the human mind? Bierce's tale of the mystery vanishings that talk about two hunters, one of whom is killed by an invisible something? The kamaitachi vacuum in Japan? Oh, come on! You must have been walking round with your eyes closed for years! It's happening all the time! People go missing, there's UFO's practically everywhere, humans spontaneously combust! Surely you must have noticed!"

Charlie shook his head. This woman was clearly bonkers. Alex wasn't so sure. That mark on his hand was still burning.

"Well, it's true. The dagger opens the portals, and without it this Mr X can just go where he wants at any time." Anya told him, putting an end to all further discussion. "Who knows, you might just get a lucky visit some day. The last person to be seen with this dagger, before you, of course, was a twelve year old girl, by the name of Grace Charlotte Beckett, some four or five years ago. Then she disappeared. There's a riddle: *to take the blood of that which stole, will open up the portal hole* . . . We thought he'd taken her. If she stole the dagger, then he needs her blood, and the dagger. And right now he has both. So, there is another world, and unless you want to end up sharing a cosy little cell with some mad-axe murderer downtown, you're going to help me find it."

"Right." added Shea. She was utterly convinced now. The marking on the boy's hand, all the weird goings on, and the murders. That's why the dagger was so valuable.

"But I stole it!" claimed Alex.

"He can't get it from you! You have to steal it from the *opposite side*! And well . . . you're a . . . a-"

"Alright!" Alex bellowed suddenly, causing the whole pub to stare. He felt panicked; this affair was rapidly spiralling out of control. They had him, hook, line and sinker. If they really knew . . .

Charlie, however, took a deep breath. No-one had ever taught him how to speak to people who were nuts. In fact he couldn't think of any job where it was taught, except perhaps at lunatic asylums. Nevertheless, he tried.

"Ladies, I don't understand why you've come here today. Unless you leave, I will be forced to call the police-"

"You? Call the police?! Oh, that's a good one!" cried Anya, looking quite mad. Didn't they were now caught in a trap, forced into realisation? They had no other option.

Alex felt quite left out of what was going on. He'd only taken them here to save his own neck, not embark on some crazy trip. Anyway, he didn't even know them; they'd just turned up at his door and demanded an explanation for his theft, like parents. Not that he had parents, but that's what he imagined them to be like. Demanding, controlling. These two certainly were. But it was a strange punishment.

Charlie sighed.

"Okay," he said quietly "We will go with you on this . . . *voyage*, then you will leave us alone, and definitely not call on me, or Alex, and you will definitely, definitely not talk any more of this stupid, ridiculous nonsense about alternate worlds. Gottit?"

Anya shrugged sweetly.

"Okay," she said.

She could get the gear. A quick phone call away there was, somewhere, a nearby warehouse, stocking everything her company could afford. They'd be ready in a week.

"See you next Tuesday then," she sang. And she got up, and walked right back out with Shea. It was set.

Alex turned to Charlie.

"You are not serious!" he cried, exploding "We are not going anywhere! They're *mad*! I only came in here with them because they were going to reveal that I'm a-"

"Alex, of course they're mad!" cried Charlie, in a voice that did not soothe, "That's the point! They're probably on drugs; ya know what some of them 'round here are like. Anyway, even if we do go with them, who knows this place better than us? We know more back alleys than you can find in Venice! Listen-two days out there with them nutcases, and they'll wander off into their own little world. It's either that or the police. And it's not like we'll ever get away from *them*, after all the things we've done! We're the most wanted this side of Aberdeen! Which do you choose?"

Alex grimaced. He really wasn't keen on it. Not often did he have the feeling of unease, but now it stole over him, like an invisible cape. It seemed he really didn't have a choice, if Charlie was going with it. In a lockup there was no way out. If he turned . . . he shuddered. It would be chaos. God only knew what would happen. He could imagine all sorts of little enquiries, tests and probes. Maybe an autopsy. He dreaded to think.

"It's nothing." said Charlie, turning back to his beer. "They're nutters. They won't be back."

How very wrong he was.

THE JOURNEY BEGINS

ONE WEEK LATER, at ten 'o' clock in the morning, four people were nearly ready to go.

Or rather, two were. A morose looking boy sat by an empty window, in a single dark living room, staring out onto the street, while a man with ginger hair stood looking dismayfully at the ruin of his living room. In the middle, two girls were checking and double-checking their list. The dusty, prawn pink floor was almost entirely covered by four rather large canvas bags; ideal for serious climbs, or holiday hikers; the sort to take on your back around the Peak District.

"What?" asked Shea, noticing Charlie's bewildered stare, as she attempted to shove a box of matches further into the canvas. "You didn't think we were gone, did you?"

Charlie watched, stunned with awe. He had no idea how they'd found him. They'd just turned up and dropped from a van, looking like they were about to tackle Kilimanjaro.

"I don't get it." he told them, for what must have been the seventh time, "What's this whole talisman thing about? I don't even know you!"

Shea rolled her eyes. How difficult plain English could be sometimes.

"You must have a short term memory." commented Anya "We've already told you all this-remember our meeting at the pub?"

"Well, yeah . . ."

"There you are then." said Anya simply. "We told you to prepare. Shea and I have been doing some research. We've got everything we need-clothes, the food, tents, all the tracking equipment. Look-"

Shea drew out a thin black device that looked like a small laptop, and opened it up. On the screen was a radius, an outline of the whole area, in a range of bizarre shades. Charlie could see his whole street, lit up in a horrid fluorescent yellow and blue.

"It's a tracker." Anya announced "We'll be able to see from the satellites where we are. We reckon it'll be okay-don't think Mr X can control the satellites. Not sure if the Ancient World even knows they exist."

Charlie stared in horror.

"But this Mr X man doesn't exist!"

"Yes, he, does." said Anya, as if talking to a small child. "Otherwise I wouldn't have spent half my life investigating them, now, would I?"

"You don't have any proof. You only showed me a book!"

"Well, then a book will have to do."

Charlie bristled.

"You cannot seriously expect me to trek half the way 'round Scotland for some psycho!"

"No?" asked Shea, standing up alongside her friend, suddenly fixing him with a steely glare. She dropped the rucksack she was holding. "Then you know the alternative. My phone's right here." She drew out the little black device. Three numbers. Your call."

Charlie felt betrayed. This wasn't what he'd had in mind. He had been more than surprised when, at half nine in the morning, they'd appeared on the doorstep, laden down with what looked like half of Millets and conceived entry.

Alex was in the corner, staring morosely out of the window. He seemed totally resigned to the challenge. Charlie knew Alex didn't have anything to lose by going-it wasn't like he had a stable nine to five. But he'd been dropped in the middle. It really was push comes to shove. There was no way he was going on a long country ramble in the middle of the cold highland, where nobody lived, away from civilisation with two women. Not a chance.

"Not going." he announced "No. You must be nuts." And he sat down, arms folded.

Shea began to dial. Three numbers. Charlie felt his stomach churn in apprehension, but he wasn't giving in.

"Hello, yes this is Shea, again. Can I speak to the Constable please? Hello, yes, it's just that I'm here with two people. Shall I tell you about them?"

Charlie suddenly changed his mind, *very* fast.

"NO!!"

He lurched across the room, trying to snatch it from her grasp, but she was surprisingly strong, and somehow managed to hold him at arms length, the little device totally out of reach.

"Coming?" she growled.

Charlie didn't know what to say. If she did call the police, it would be the end of days. He didn't much care for prison systems, but he would probably, with the sheer number of deals he'd done, get a good year.

"Fine." He pulled back, and Shea lowered her arm.

"You owe me, remember? I nearly lost my job because of you! That dagger was the most expensive thing we've had in a long time. It was entrusted to *me*! Do you know how stupid I felt, trying to explain that the shop had been robbed in my first two months of being there?! Do you know how ashamed that made me feel?! You might not have morals, but I do! I thought Mr Finchley's heart was going to break! So now I'm going to get it back! And *you're* going to help me!"

She turned away, back to the phone. Charlie waited with bated breath.

"Yes, sorry about that. I thought it was something important. Turns out it's not. No. No, that's fine. Thank you. Bye."

She closed her phone, bent down, and carried on packing so they couldn't see her face. Inside, Shea was seething. She had lost her whole reputation because of him, and that boy.

It wasn't like they even had a choice! The least they could do was help pack!

On the other side of the room, Charlie collapsed into a chair, and watched them, his gaze becoming unfocused. He was imagining all the heavy climbing they'd have to do. He'd never really been one for long, strenuous exercise; an hour at the gym, fine. But not *days* of just walking about. That would become *so* BORING! He slouched, thinking moodily about this, with the rustle of plastic and clatter of various items, as they were checked and repacked. Several times one of them disappeared out the room, returning with something of his, but he made no protest. He would, inevitably, end up using it, as he had no choice but to go. Shimmers of light coloured the window in yellow, and something bright swung, and caught his eye. Charlie blinked back to life, trying to see what it was. In front of him, Shea bent down, her back to him, and turned, something swaying across her neck that caught the light, glinting a bright silver. It looked like a sort of Celtic cross, a red diamond twinkling in the middle that caught and burnt his eyes.

"What's *that?*"

Shea looked blankly at him, then down at her chest, to where Charlie was pointing.

"Oh, that. Just an amulet. Meant to be magical. Gives you a feeling, y'know, like if you're in danger."

"Oh." Charlie settled back down. Nothing special then. Just folk tales. A mystical belief. Anya was, for some reason, packing the wolf talisman. Charlie could see its dark metallic shape, and ruby red eye.

"Why do we need that?" he asked.

Alex looked up and started sharply from his place, and in the yellow sunlight Charlie caught a glimpse of the red scar on his hand. He wondered how long it would take to heal. He didn't know much about Alex's kind, and Alex had never been one to bring it up. From what he could gather of the early months they had spent together, until Charlie had got Alex his own place in a rough 'n' cut deal, was that Alex had been the way he was since around the age of five. The family had been on holiday somewhere, and Alex had been bitten. His parents had found him the next morning, crying and shaking on the sodden ground, and took him immediately to the nearest doctor, who told them of the boy's rare and incurable condition. Charlie wondered if they had been angry; he had never had children himself, but Alex was almost like a son to him; a son that was growing up. Alex had been grateful for the hospitality, and Charlie, reluctant to make him move on, had hired the lad in order to help with the work. Appearing as a surly adolescent, Alex had proved to be quick and nimble; possibly qualities of his nature. The problem was though, despite his neat abilities, Alex did have one drawback.

Turning. It had been terrible to begin with; Charlie had fitted locks of every description onto the door of his spare room; trying to barricade the beast in. Lost in the dead of night he would cower, shaking, under his bedclothes, his own door barricaded from the inside, listening to the blood-curling screams and sobbing, punctuated by vicious snapping and growling, then a blood-curdling howl. Several times people would knock on the door to complain, not realising the danger they were in, and Charlie had had to insist it was somebody's dog that he kept once every month to make them go away. "What'd ya keeping, a rottweiler?!" they'd demand, furious. Worse still was when they threatened to go to the police. Charlie had always managed to stop them, promising it wouldn't happen the next night, but things had begun to get desperate. It had taken time, but Charlie had learnt that by keeping raw meat on the floor, the monster kept relatively quiet. Alex had slowly learnt to control himself, even now to the point that he could turn when he wanted, and, so long as it wasn't full moon, kept relatively humanised. Charlie had spent many evenings before now, watching the racing, sitting side by side with a hairy, elongated adolescent. Still, it was a risky business: Charlie was concerned what would happen if anyone found out. That was why they'd had to move him away, closer to the forest, so he could run as and when he pleased. And now these two had, and they knew. It was lucky they were educated. Anya seemed to at least know what a werewolf was, and there was no point trying to hide that mark upon Alex's palm. At least she hadn't gone off her head and called the RSPCA, or the cops, or whoever it was people called when they found out their town was inhabited by a hulking, great, man-eating werewolf.

"I think we're ready." called Shea. She straightened up and stretched. So did Anya. They looked at the boys.

Charlie sighed.

"Fine." he said. It seemed like fate had spoken for him. Anya threw him a backpack, and, gaping at its size, he hauled it on. It weighed a ton. What the hell had she packed in there? The kitchen sink? And where were his boots? And why was Alex acting like he couldn't be bothered if they were going with nutters or not?

With very little choice, the two men stood, stumbling beneath their sudden weights. It was time to go. Anya beckoned them out, and Charlie, grumbling, shut and locked the door behind him that led to his sweet little abode. Then they set off, down the garden path and out of the gate, tailing their way in an unhappy line down the high-street, heading into the moors of Scotland, out into the unknown.

THE FIRST LEG

"I . . . CAN'T . . . DO . . . this . . . *anymore.*"

Anya was lying on the ground, sweat running down her face. She was tired and hungry, not to mention absolutely desperate for water.

"Have another one." Shea told her, offering some of the energy tablets they had taken with them. "I'll do you good."

Anya took one wearily. She should have got fitter before she set out. The idea was good, the practice was proving a little more tricky. Now her fitness was really letting her down. So far they'd spent the first day together, and covered, Anya guessed, a good eight miles. The tracker had been packed, and showed about eleven. Fair enough. The bags were proving desperately heavy, and they'd only covered the long, winding gravel path leading out into the distance, strewn on either side with grand fir trees, towering high. It was like being in the army. Alex and Charlie had trailed behind them, making little conversation, only when asked. It seemed like they had conserved their energy; something Anya supposed they should have done a little more of. Next to her, Shea was sitting down. She too was suffering, but not as much. She checked her watch. It was half past four. It would go dark by five. They needed to get to the end.

Wearily Anya got up. Her muscles ached but she didn't want the boys to see. Her rucksack was bending her forth, making her appear slightly shrunken as she took its weight. How did people *do* these things? Why did they even want to? Still, there was only half an hour to go.

They moved on. Around them, darkness began to slowly descend, bringing temperatures much colder than they'd noticed in the town. Perhaps it was just knowing they'd be on their own for the night, wrapped up in sleeping bags, rather than in a sweet, comfy bed. Charlie shivered. Behind him, Alex noticed and said nothing. Humans were prone to the cold; most warm-blooded things were. As for himself, he didn't feel it as much. That at least, was an advantage. As for pitching in a tent, there was no worry there either; Alex had spent time sleeping in a variety of peoples' beds that were meant to be 'his own.' As long as no-one said "This is where you'll be.", Alex could settle down pretty much anywhere and call it home. Just so long as it was his choice.

The black trees became less and less noticeable as twilight turned to grey, then a shade of black. The stars came out, but they were so far apart that barely anyone took notice, apart from Alex, who cast around, gazing for the moon.

They decided to set up camp. Tents, green and with just enough room for two, were laid out and erected. Then, without saying much, the two teams split-boys and girls, as they settled down for the night.

The next day, everyone woke pretty early, and they'd reached the end of the trail by nine, looking out onto large, open grassland, that seemed to belong to no-one, and be used for nothing. It had been odd waking up with complete strangers, and everyone had got dressed and eaten, pretty much within the privacy of their own tent. No-one was talking much yet.

They began to cross, walking through fences and over grass, until the trail could no longer be seen. Then they hit a forest, and new evergreens sprang up, immersing them in a confusion of shadows as they navigated their way forth. They walked on, into the morning, stopping only in the middle for lunch, where it was packet chicken and rice all round, cooked on a trangia stove. Then it was off again. By nightfall the shadows blurred their tired senses. Heavy straps cut into shoulders, and set up was slow. They had still not come to the edge. Wrapped up tightly in their sleeping bags, tiredness sent them into a second quiet night. Only Alex lay awake, longing for the outside world that invaded the tent with its fresh scent of earthy ground, listening for the squirrels, as their scented flesh passed through the trees above.

THE ARGUMENT

B Y THE THIRD day, it was like walking in the Arctic. As soon as they stepped out of the forest, snow appeared, lying thick on the ground. It was like trudging through an ice sheet. Anya was glad they'd brought boots. The walk had been quiet; odd flakes falling here and there on the empty plateau.

Before long they had come into view. Mountains loomed before them; the great peaks of an unknown range that Anya had briefly warned them about. They were a long way off, but something was warning her-an odd sort of feeling she couldn't quite explain. Pulling the scarf from her mouth, Anya turned her back on the wind to ask Shea to consult the tracker. On the screen, the radius showed four yellow dots. There didn't appear to anything else around.

Anya hesitated, and the group paused, watching the bright eyes barely visible against the scarf she had pulled against whitened cheeks. It was her duty to tell them. If anything was to go awry . . . well, there were only four of them. If they were travelling on mass, they'd have better protection, for one thing, and it might not actually matter so much if they lost one or two here and there. But four? They just couldn't afford it. Vigilance was crucial here on such snowy plains, where the barren whiteness and cold lethargy could turn your brain to numbness, wiping your thoughts, turning you into a walking target.

"Be careful!" she warned, stopping the group in their tracks. "This is where it'll be interesting. This is where the Red Caps will be. If you see anything, shout right away. We'll have to use some of the energy I stored to transport us out of danger."

Charlie's eyes fixed on the round, orange gadget affixed to Anya's forearm. *That's* what it was-well, she could have said. What if they been got before now, and she hadn't told them? As if that would have been good for him!

Alex, keeping his eyes peeled, and knowing damn well what Red Caps looked like, focused his glare to a greater intensity. On the mountains, he could see every crag if he looked, but no Red Caps. In fact, apart from themselves, he could not detect the presence of a single living creature. He drew breath. Mmm; nothing there, just Shea's sweet smell; Anya smelling like old paper and worn leather. There was sweat, and a strange smell of nylon on skin, coming from Charlie close in his right. Alex stepped forward, trying to free himself from the other's stench, and sniffed again. No, the air was clear.

"Oh, man," Shea was saying. "How come we have to come into contact with creatures from the underworld so soon? They're such stupid creatures, wanting to take over everything. They never do any good."

Something touched a sensitive chord, making Alex wheel around.

"You think I don't know what you mean when you say creatures?" he growled, angrily. "We're not all bad!"

"I didn't say that." Shea protested, "I just said that not all of them are for the good of this world. Come on, Alex! If you *are* what you say you are, well, you can't exactly say you're natural!"

Silence descended on the troubled crew, and they stared out at the icy region that lay before them. Mountains loomed like sleeping giants. All was white, bleak, directionless. It felt as though they'd fallen into heaven. The light was bright, a constant brightness, like a torch beaming in your eyes, illuminating the vast scale of their destination. It was cold, bitterly so, and Shea felt like she had when she was three, wrapped up in scarf, coat and every jumper she could find, protecting her. Everyone else was wrapped up too. Charlie's face was hardly visible, save for the snow goggles he wore, allowing watery eyes to peep out across the giant land. Alex though he looked ridiculous.

"How far away are we?" he asked.

"Twenty two miles."

The crew stood in silence once more. Twenty two miles? Twenty two miles across lakes and mountains, and god knows what?

"Well," started Shea, picking up her backpack. "I suppose this isn't going to get us anywhere. Come on. If this Mr X is really here, we can't exactly wait around."

The gang dejectedly picked up their bags. Shea stumbled in the snow under the weight of food and clothing, tools and tent.

"Darn!" she muttered.

To her right, Alex ignored her; he wasn't exactly in a good mood. As far as he was concerned she had insulted him and named him as black as those they were now about to face.

Really, whose side was she on?! He didn't even know why he was left waiting for them either; he was faster, stronger than them. He could probably get there in half the time, if not less. Yet here he was, waiting around for some stupid complaining human, who thought he was the bad one! Well, he could do without that.

It was another five miles before they reached the bottom of the snow-ridden crags. Looking up, Charlie could not see how anyone could possibly even dream of wanting to go climbing. Still he had no choice. It was already twenty miles back. And he wasn't about to go anywhere alone.

Together they climbed. Tightropes, and harnesses strained under their weight as they ascended the snowy mountains. Presently, the temperature dropped until only Alex could feel his fingers, clutching gingerly at the snow-ridden rock. It was tough, and the silence that grew as they ascended was almost formidable in its presence. If one of them fell now, Anya thought, looking down at the snow-pile beneath them, she doubted they would be found this side of the century. And the Red Caps were still out there. Who knew when they would meet one? She didn't think she had the strength to carry on. Her fingers were cold and numb, her shoulders screaming for a rest. Aching muscles gripped her thoughts; she would at least tear a ligament. She looked across. Alex was helping Shea, hauling her up each time, as though her entire weight consisted of nothing more than her backpack. It wasn't Alex's choice, she knew, particularly after what had just been said. It certainly hadn't been very tactful. Stretching out her fingers to the white, her mind wandered; was Shea still in doubt about Alex's alter-form? And if so, why? Mind you, as far as Shea was concerned, Alex was still a thief; still bottom of the pile, but, still, it hadn't been a good time to suggest so. Actually, she was surprised Alex hadn't refused to help outright-their climb was filled with an iciness that had nothing to do with the weather. On the other side, Charlie too was hauling himself up the mountain. His face was red with the effort.

Anya looked upwards. A long thin plateau stretched upwards to a palid sky. The mountain seemed to grow. She shook herself. *'Just don't look up'* she told herself firmly, trying to inch her frozen fingers to the next ledge, arm outstretched, pale snow scattering on her cheeks. *'Don't even look up. And for God's sake, don't look down.'*

Looking down was the worst thing she could do, and though it was difficult, she wasn't prepared to fail. They had twenty-two miles to go-twenty-two! God, her insides nearly gave up at the thought.

"Hurry up, Anya." Alex growled, ten feet above, Shea dangling from the rope attached to his arm, her hands clutching the snow-covered sides. Anya sighed, and hauled her protesting body upwards. *Just keep going,* she told herself, *Don't stop now.*

Eventually, after more than an hour's climb, they reached the top. A great barrier of snow stretched before them like an icy carpet. Shea, hauled up first by Alex, grinned in a rather dazed fashion and began to search in her backpack, looking for her PC. The light was even brighter up here. Just the ideal place to get a good signal, and a bit of power. The sky wasn't too bad either. Looking at it now, they weren't likely to be snowed upon for at least the next two hours.

Alex had recovered quickly, in fact particularly so for someone who had just completed a one hour climb. Shea could tell he was interested; he was looking at her laptop in a bemused sort of way, and she could tell by his expression that curiosity was getting the better of him. Mind you, if he wanted to know, he had a tongue: he'd have to ask. She knew he would.

"What's that?" he barked, peering over her shoulder at the hand-size device.

"A laptop."

"What? *That* small?"

"Yep."

"Isn't it going to run out of juice?"

"Nope," replied Shea, wielding it around, checking for any signs of life. "Solar. Or lunar. Or wind. It can use pretty much any energy it can find. Except for rain, of course, never rain power. I've got the generator too, if we get really stuck-it's just in my bag. My boss, Mr Finchley, showed me how. Really it's just about energy conversion. Solar, lunar and wind energy can all be converted to kinetic energy. That charges the battery."

She waved the device in mid-air. Behind them, Anya climbed over the ledge and slumped on the ground, trying to recover. She was so exhausted she thought she would collapse. Tiredness pulled at every muscle, making her want to cry out. Not that she had the energy. She knew they would never be easy, but that mountain was harder to climb than she'd ever expected.

"How far?" she heard herself asking.

"Twenty . . . well, twenty. Just under. Yeah." Shea replied, completely her, looking about at the landscape before them. An icy cavern of mountains lay stretched like sleeping giants. Anya groaned. She couldn't even get up. She closed her eyes. She might as well sleep there. Then she felt a hand round her waist, and she was hauled to her feet.

"Come on." said Alex softly. Anya looked at him balefully. Looking at what he was wearing, she could not believe he wasn't cold. Well, she wasn't cold either. In fact she was dripping with sweat, running in rivulets, trapped inside the many layers she had hauled on that morning. It would be a miracle if she ever got them off-she guessed they must be glued together. Worst thing you could do, really; taking them off here. In such conditions, any sudden change in temperature could easily shock the system, and they were a long way from any medical help now.

"We've got a long way to go."

Anya stumbled. Her brain went fuzzy, headachy with the white light, She tried to stand. She was so tired. She couldn't, possibly, go on. It was impossible. She wasn't built for this. She was meant to be back in London, at a meeting. Or at home, feet up, nursing a nice mug of tea.

She closed her eyes and swayed, taking in the silence, but when she opened them only the vast mountain region stretched before her once more. Shea was holding her computer up in the air as if trying to find a signal, Alex looking over her shoulder. They seemed to have hauled Charlie up, who was sitting, knees up, in the snow. Both were completely ignoring her. She felt bruised and betrayed. Only Charlie seemed to have noticed that anything was wrong, and even he wasn't running to her rescue. He had pulled off his backpack, and still sitting, was slowly unrolling a sleeping bag.

"What'ya doin'?" asked Anya, not caring if she slurred her words.

"Preparation." Charlie answered. He sounded tired, and began once again looking through his backpack. Anya seriously wanted to lie down. She didn't think her legs could take any more. She was going to pass out.

"I wouldn't do that yet." Shea told Charlie, looking up. "We're not staying here for long."

Anya gave up, and sat down in the snow. Dressed in long waterproofs, she only felt a cold numbness in her aching thighs as the snow touched gortex.

"I know. Just checkin' summit."

Anya didn't bother to ask what it was he was checking. She lay down on the cold surface. Presently she began to feel a little better, as if the cold air here cleared her senses. The sun was quite warm, now it was shining through. Anya was glad. She needed sun too.

Shea was busy, looking at the map. The north was just a barren land and at least she had her laptop to help navigate their way across. Mind you, that wasn't so simple either–it's wasn't like she could see every dip and dent of the mountain, and if they didn't plan properly, it might be one of these that stopped them in their tracks, or even caused a death. She was grateful for Alex's help-in truth there was no way she'd have made it up herself, though this wasn't a fact she was about to admit to yet. She turned, and saw Anya lying on the frozen ground. The girl looked drained. Suddenly she realised just how hard it must have been, and how much of the work Alex must have been doing. Gosh. She hadn't realised that it might be so damned hard, let alone near impossible. She turned. Charlie was still unrolling his sleeping bag on the cold ground.

"Don't do that." Shea called, again. Unrolling your dry kit and getting it cold and wet was the worst thing you could do. Hypothermia, exhaustion, weight loss, altitude sickness could all have you crawling back to your sleeping bag for days if not longer, and that was if you survived. Beautiful though it was, this was Death Valley. Dare to take your dripping coat off for one second, and you were exposing your whole body to a multitude of issues. The breeze, though it didn't feel cold, probably was. That numbed you in situations like these; numbed even your brain, tricked you. As she watched, Charlie lifted something out of his bag.

"What's that?" Shea asked.

"The amulet." Charlie replied, holding the gleaming metal up to the light. "Your one."

"Why?"

"Just want to know if you're getting any vibes from it."

"I don't get *vibes*." Shea replied sarcastically, almost surprised she still had strength to muster some. "I'm no physcic, y'know."

"Well, just in case he wants someone to 'do a little bidding.'"

Charlie held the amulet out to her in one black gloved hand.

"Fine." Shea snatched the gleaming hulk of diamond off him, and held it up to the light. She was a little annoyed. She'd checked it not three hours ago, and they couldn't wait to get sidetracked by Red Caps, or, even worse, let them know where they were. The less contact they had with it the better. The little red dial swung like a pendulum, vibrating slightly.

"OW!" she cried, dropping the amulet on the icy ledge.

"What?!"

Everyone looked confused. Even Charlie had dropped his pack and come rushing to her side. Shea held her arm out.
"It shocked me!" she cried.
"What do you mean?" asked Charlie, reaching out to pick the amulet off the floor, but Shea put her foot on it.
"Don't touch it!" she said, warningly. "I don't know what that shock means. For all I know, he might know we're here now!"

Shea saw the blood drain from the others faces as they looked at each other in panic. Oops, she thought. She shouldn't have said that.

"Well, he might . . . but not necessarily. All I'm saying is that we should take care."

Anya, sat up, and dizzily shook her head. No, they needed to set off again-now! If Mr X did know where they were this was definitely not a good place to stay. When Shea had clothed the amulet to dampen any signals it may be giving off or receiving, and everyone had recovered sufficiently, they were ready to scale down the second side of the mountain. This was a great deal easier than climbing. All they had to do was stick their picks in the ground, and lower themselves from their ropes, gradually. It would have been easier if they could fly, or just abseil from peak to peak, but as none of them could, this was their only real option. Alex went last, taking the picks and ropes attached to them off, to be reused once the others had descended, and dropping so quickly he was almost a flash. Anya thought he was showing off a bit, but none of the others seemed to mind. At the bottom of the mountain lay an icy sheet spreading far into the fog. The sun was starting to go in again, and everyone could tell that if they didn't find shelter soon, they could be exposing themselves to a particularly violent storm. They all knew that winds in the Arctic could blow up to a speed of three hundred miles per hour-that was something they had researched, and none of them felt particularly willing to be caught in such a breeze. What the winds could blow here was unknown-it was not perhaps Arctic tundra, but across such a wide spanning area, with nothing to block them, channelled between the mountains, Anya was willing to bet they could be pretty strong. Gale force, in fact. The icy sheet looked impossible to judge, melting away into fog and an icy mist. Their breath rose in icy jets from their mouths. Hurriedly they put their snow skis on, hooked up, they were ready. Anya wasn't particularly looking forward to this. The mountain climb had sapped most of her energy, and it would be a little while yet before her glucose drink began to kick in. She was tired, but knew they must go on. Staying here was the worst thing they could do.

A race against time, she thought.

They set off, dragging their aching bodies across the icy layer. There was little conversation, and before long they were stranded, trudging wearily in a white mist. Their situation looked hopeless, but Shea kept checking her laptop, so Anya hoped they would be fine. Charlie was silent and huddled behind her. Usually, she had found, the first to complain, Charlie kept unusually quiet, and this occupied Anya's thoughts the whole time they trudged on and on, into the wilderness. That and the Red Caps. After trekking for what seemed to be miles and miles, and hours and hours, with many a torturous thought rattling around their brains they came to an icy standstill.

At last something loomed out of the nothingness. In the blurring white Anya nearly fainted with happiness. Her mind had become dulled, her thoughts torturous and demeaning, horrid visions of what lay before them swimming meaninglessly round her brain while she forced her aching thighs to trudge on. The icy glacier rose twenty, no, wait, thirty, no, wait, *fifty* feet ahead of them, and her thoughts quickly turned. *God*, thought Anya in dismay. How could she ever scale that? This trip was surely a death trap. Mr X or even she had lured them there, and they were all going to die of starvation or exhaustion, with no-one to know and no-one to care.

She couldn't believe the situation she had gotten herself into. This was totally mad! What on earth were they doing, thinking they could beat one of the old ones, with nothing more than a tracker, to help?! They were surely mad, all of them! She just couldn't believe it, the whiteness, the numbness.

She was hungry too. Why didn't they just get a helicopter, like Shea'd said? That had been her idea not to, and she was the one leading them there! For the first time, Anya began to really question her motives. She wasn't meant to be doing this-Shea was the fighter, and Alex, well, Alex was just Alex, who could turn around and kill her if he liked. She was just a researcher, really, nothing big. Why Charlie had agreed to come with them, now puzzled her too. After all, he was probably *better off* in a prison cell! It wasn't like he had much to offer—just human strength and a bit of a complaint to liven up conversation. Oh well, at least his personality was keeping her in good enough humour. If it wasn't for him she'd probably be suicidal by now. The whiteness pressing down upon them was ominous; nature's great reel of never-ending discouragement. They shouldn't have come-none of them. She should have contacted her people and left them to deal with it, but *no*, she hadn't. She'd just upped and gone without a second thought. Big mistake.

The ledge was now right in front of them. With a silent sigh of relief, Shea, close at the front, realised it had a cave. Just as her laptop had said; well thank god for that. Relief. Rest. Sleep. That was what she needed. Surely Anya couldn't expect them to go on. They stopped. Shea untied the rope that attached her to the group, slid blindly up to the cave, and pulling it out of her pack, began waving her thin laptop around the edge, obviously searching. Anya groaned internally. She didn't care much for danger any more. Just to get out of the blinding whiteness and to get inside was all she wanted to do. It had started to snow, great icy flakes raining down on their shoulders from an unseen height.

Finally Shea stopped checking whatever it was she had been looking for.

"It's safe." she announced.

Thank God! thought Anya, and she began trudging her way wearily towards the monstrous cavern. Alex's arm brushed hers, but she barely took notice. The cave looked like the most inviting thing she'd seen for hours. How <u>could</u> she have made it this far? Shea was already inside, and she knew Charlie was right behind her, squinting in his snow goggles up to the white light.

Silently the crew trudged inside, their boots and snow skis clanging on the bare rock floor. The interior decoration wasn't brilliant either; brown. *Great, boring*, thought Anya, *but my God, at least it's dry.*

Alex had walked in too. There were no places to perch, and he was now sitting on the cold ground, removing his skis. Anya bent down and removed hers too, then collapsed on the cold stone surface.

"A fire." called Charlie, whipping out some matches and some firepaper. Anya didn't see how he did it, but before long there were long roaring flames the centre of the cave and the crew sat, in almost total silence, thawing their numbed limbs. It was a painful process, but gradually each could feel the life returning to them, like a burden lifted. Then talk began. Shea whipped out her laptop once more and began to show them their path. They had a long way to go-over four more mountains, across a lake, then across another two before they finally reached the castle, before they even began their fight.

"How long will it take?" Alex wanted to know. Shea drew up a weather map. "Looking at the forecasts, we'll lose two or three days at Mount Fior. We'll camp here-" she pointed at the screen "-in that cave. It's safe as far as I know, but if not, we'll have to stop for at least five days here, at this cave, on the bottom of Lake Logan. That's not really ideal though."

"Why not?"

"Tell you when we get there."

The night was passed unceremoniously, each sleeping in his or her own dreams of how they might separate the ominous Mr. X from their land. Alex dreamed of a fight, for, as strong as he was, he never missed an opportunity to show off. He knew in reality they couldn't do that, but he wouldn't have minded another chance to show he *could* be the hero, and at least prove Shea wrong. He seemed to be coping the best out of all of them, he thought-nature had made it easier for him to climb, crawl, walk—anything to do with sport or movement really. And here he could be who he truly wanted to be. Looking at the fact that as a werewolf, this was meant to be a bad thing, and his alter personality made to ruin his life, Alex could gratefully reflect that, in total, it hadn't paid off too badly.

Anya was flat out on the cold stone floor. Deep in sleep, she dreamt of storms and walking, waking only to realise that this was in fact reality. A new white light lit the cave, not so different from yesterdays. She groaned. How crazy that she should have dreamt of this, when sleep was supposed to give her rest! Sitting up, she was pleased to feel that most of the fatigue from yesterday had drained away, and though not 100% better; her muscles did at least feel less taught. Her head felt clearer too. She supposed this was what it was-the mental stableness. Not letting your thoughts run away with you, but not burdening them either. It was a difficult task. So Anya spent the next thirty minutes thinking of all the things she could think of that would keep her mind occupied on this barren landscape. There really wasn't much stimulus. She didn't even have one of those Polka Game Cubes that she could play on while walking. She wished she'd taken hers with her. She took a bet that Alex would have one, somewhere. He seemed like the kind of boy who would spend alot of time doing nothing.

Just at that moment Alex stirred. He seemed to be deep in sleep, and Anya wondered how he did it.

A NASTY SURPRISE

B REAKFAST, AT LEAST, was a hearty-ish affair. The fire had run out, and though they had plenty left, Shea had said she didn't want to waste any more fire paper. Charlie and the others suspected that this might be in case they got stuck, and they sat in silence, drinking their glucose solution pro-power drinks.

Once again they set off into the blinding wilderness. Anya's goggles pressed against her skin and began to steam up, making her instantly want to remove them. She knew she couldn't-UV levels were high in these regions, the light bouncing off the pearly whiteness, and getting snow or ice in her eye was not worth the risk. Let that happen, and you could go with partial sight, or even end up blind. Even if it wasn't snowing, you could still lose a fair bit of water from the exposed pupil with the wind chill. And then, if your eye went numb, or you forgot to blink, it would begin to freeze over without you even realising.

Still, she didn't like the swaddled feeling. She was sweaty inside, with the cool air pushing past her many layers, making her want to throw them off. They trudged on, and on, and on. It would take the whole day to meander through three more mountains, eventually stopping for the night at the bottom of Mount Fior. The storms were getting worse; gusts billowing into icy gales, picking up snow that blew constantly in their faces, and obscured the already meaningless landscape. They'd walked in a fog for most of the day. Anya was running out of things to think of; her brain began to dwell on the difficult and risky task ahead of her, making time go even slower. Every second seemed like an hour, every hour like a day. Her ears were cold, so much so, that she could barely feel them, the sides of her head were starting to numb as they reached the icy glacier at the bottom of the mountain. The storm had grown worse. Snow ran past them in sheets. They could barely see one another-at times it seemed like each was walking totally alone, separate from all contact, tied to a bobbing rope that led no-where, instead of to the person in front. In the storm, the cave they found was very much like the first; cold, bare meaningless. The crew again ate a silent glucose tea, and slept upon the cold and grey floor while the wind whipped at the entrance, creating gusts that would have made them toss and turn had they not been so tired.

By the fifth day, it was a push to reach the lake. The wind had died down, and after spending four days of total mind-numbing boredom in which all they could do was talk or sleep, everyone was desperate to push on. Even Charlie had run out of conversation almost, and had spent a great deal of time packing and re-packing his bag, checking his equipment and supplies over and over again. The only break in the day was breakfast and tea, when each was allowed their pro-power gel. Taking no more than a minute to consume, however, each was left to suck it slowly, and they were discouraged from any physical exertion, meaning most of the time they just lay in their sleeping bags in a half stupor, and talked meaninglessly of this and that. Any sign of relenting, and the wind would soon pick back up, dashing any hopes of setting off again.

Finally the wind died down, bringing the snow almost to a standstill. The motley crew gazed out into the bleak whiteness. Anya was kitted up, Charlie was too, as was Alex. Shea was checking her laptop.

"Right." she announced, bringing them to all clamour around the screen. "We are *here*. We need to reach here. It's going to be a tough trek, but the wind is only at twenty knots at the minute. This means we can make it over Snafell Point by nightfall, and cross the lake by morning if we need to. I'd rather not chance it trying to reach the other side and not get over the mountain."

Here she opened another file with a picture of a grotesque looking thing on it.

'Cthulu', it was entitled.

"The Cthulu is a weird animal." Shea informed them. "It's body is kind of like a zebra, but with a snake's neck, a dragon's tail and dragon's claws. There's another ground version called a Genther. It's like a talking panther, but it's got black and white stripes. It's fierce and deadly, and can leap at you at any moment. But that is nothing compared to this. This is big-dragon sized big. With talons, feathers, stripes, points, you name it. They will rip us to shreds if we wake them. This is my plan-"

"Wait-them?" asked Alex, bemused, pointing at the screen. "How many are there?"

"Well, we don't know." Shea sighed. "Unfortunately, anyone who's ever tried to track these things have, y'know-" she drew a finger across her neck.

"Anyway, these might be different; there are several versions,"-she drew up several images—"like this one, here. See? It's like a dragon, but with a bird's tail. This one has a lion's tail, and a horse's head. It happens because they all cross-breed with one another. Legend has it that it was a lion mating with a snake, then that mated with a horse, and a bird and a snake mated too, so that's why there are several different versions. All of them are very dangerous. They have good sight and sharp claws, so we'll need to shut up and hide. The only way we can even hope to get across the lake is by raft when they're all asleep, or to get on one."

The others looked at each other.

"So . . . is there no other way?" Alex asked.

"Not really, not unless we learn to fly, and they don't mind chasing small birds. I suppose we could take the invisibility potion I got us from Finchley's, but that only lasts for half an hour, and to be honest, I don't actually-no offense to believers, Anya—think it *is* invisibility potion. And I definitely don't want to try it out now. We only have three bottles in any case. So if we take one that'll keep each of us covered for thirty minutes. After that, it's anything from twenty to forty minutes to the other side if we walk around, then up the mountain. Personally I suggest we fly, but we'll somehow have to control one."

"Most likely they're bound by Mr. X too.", Anya added. "They may even know we're here. If you see anything unusual about them let me know, but they're always on the lookout for food anyway, and four juicy humans won't go amiss. They'll be able to smell us from miles off across open waters."

"Can we really do this?" asked Alex. "Because, personally, if they are 'bound', or even hungry, I don't think they'll be too willing just to serve as a free taxi service. I can't see how we'll do it."

Charlie held up the talisman. He waiting, swinging it in mid-air until the gleaming diamond flashed and caught their eye. It had worked.

"With this." he said, nodding to Shea. "This necklace; well, yours, Shea, is meant to be very powerful. At the very least it's very bright. If we blind them as they come near, we might be able to direct them to do *our* bidding. Is that right?"

"Right." said Shea. "This thing is something I've been looking at for days. Since it's been in our presence, it's kind of got used to us. The bond from Mr X is still there, but there is only one of him, and he is far away. There are four of us, and we are close. It kind of feels out personality-a remote control if you like. I've done some research. The further the Red-Caps are, the harder they must be to control. That's why they didn't stay to kill Alex; one-because they weren't told to, but two, because he summoned them back before they could realise what was happening to them. I reckon if you'd have stayed, Alex, he wouldn't have been able to control them the way he did. Someone would have come back for you, and *not* in a good way."

"So this thing . . ." said Anya slowly, puzzling, causing the group to stare in alarm at her hesitancy. "Does it really work? I mean, no offense Shea, but is it real? I know I had a look at it before, and it seems real, but have you *used* it before? And can it control big things? Coz judging from everything I know about them, Cthulus *aren't* small."

Alex's eyes nearly popped out of his head. *She wasn't sure?!*

Shea grimaced. "I *have* tried it before, but only for a set time. It says here Cthulus are strong, both in mind and body. They'll have to be all four of us on one. And even then it'll be only just under our control, I hope. In my research I found, well, it says here, if it's eaten recently, it'll be too strong."

"So how do we know which ones have eaten?"

"Rather more, the question is, how do we tell the one's that haven't eaten? Well, simple. They'll be the ones who are flying towards us the fastest."

"Like leading a mouse to some cheese." pondered Charlie, thoughtfully, in the background.

"Well, yes, kind of. Once we get to the lake we only want to attract one. The hardest part will be on the ledge. If we're not careful they'll see us. I've got thermal imaging on here, so we'll hopefully be able to climb down when they're sleepy, or some are feeding. If they don't move, they're not too active. That'll make it safer for us."

"At the bottom Charlie will hold this out. They can feel vibes. Some of the smaller ones will come to investigate. Hopefully, that's when we'll put one under. Then we'll go over the lake and the mountain, with any luck."

"If not?"

"Err, well, then . . . I guess . . . we're doomed. There's no other chance we have."

"Great."

The crew looked at each other.

"So . . . there really is no other way?" Alex asked, again. "Couldn't we have done this whole façade by plane or helicopter? It'd save alot of death traps."

Shea gazed at him like he was stupid. "I said that at first, but if you actually *think* . . . . A helicopter is so noisy Mr X would know we're coming from miles off. You really think you can cross a lake in a big metal bird with these things, huh? Sure it'd be easier, but it's a plain death trap, and it's just so obvious it's unreal. That's why!"

Alex shrugged, hurt. "S'just an idea." he muttered.

Charlie was at the entrance. He was raring to go. If he really was going to die, well, then he'd better get on with it. Put it this way, if this was really how the odds stood, he'd rather die soon from one of these Cthulu things than from perishing slowly out in the cold. They were taking far too long as it was.

"Come on then!" he called, "Are we setting off or what?"

The others hastened to him, Shea beckoning them on. "If we don't go now, night will fall before we reach Mount Snafell Cave! The lake's just behind it!" she called. "And that really is a death trap!"

So once out of the cave they began yet another weary trek and climb. The mountain seemed even larger than the last, though incredibly, they managed to make the climb in under fifty minutes. Then they abseiled down, and walked for another four hours in blinding fog, searching hopelessly as they trudged for the white peak that was Mount Snafell.

The cool breeze that blew gained force, blowing snow in their faces, threatening to tear their packs and hurl them across the frost-bitten wilderness, back from where they'd come.

"Come on!" urged Shea as it began to pick up, howling in gusts around them. "There's no cave here! We've got to go on!"

Together they climbed, billowing gusts snatching about them, teasing them, laughing as they struggled on. Several times it threatened to blow them clear off the mountain, and they clung to the slipping ice, praying to stay on, the wind pulling and tugging with icy claws.

Shea stared upwards as she gripped the rock face, fingers numb, knees scraped and bruised from the ice as she forced them upwards. "Come on!" she urged, again, "Not far now! Then we can abseil down!"

But the wind whipped her words away, and they were lost to the storm.

Monsters And Demons

THE LAKE WAS a vast ocean of cold-looking water, bluer than the icy mists they had so far encountered. Behind that, smothered by a screen of cold, lay the mountains, tall and gangling, ready and waiting to hold them back. Charlie groaned. They hadn't prepared for this. There was no boat, no other means of crossing. All that was left lay the dangerous task before them.

Looking about on the icy precipice, every inch of Shea's rationale was telling her to turn back. This was dangerous. It would be the most dangerous thing they did. The lake was full of ancient monsters, protectors of the ancient sites; almost like dragons, with the same deadliness and temper.

Well, she thought, *at least they had made it so far.* On the icy ledge and out of sight, it was her decision to sit and rest. There had to be recuperation before they tried to cross it. Otherwise, they'd never make it alive.

About an hour must have passed. Hidden from view, Shea had fallen almost into a trance-like sleep. She was soon woken.

A poisonous scream rent the air, loud and terrifying. Shea scrambled to her feet, awake in a second.

What the hell was going on?!

Stretching out before her, across the rippling lake, a Cthulu stood, wings outstretched, pain in its eyes, as Alex jammed her pendant into its vision, carefully holding it aloft. Another gut-wrenching scream hit the air. It hovered like a blinded bird, wings beating like an eagle in mid flight, its ghastly black hide scaly and hard to climb. It rose, speeding across the vast ocean, its eyes wide and dazed under the spell.

"Look out!" cried Shea. There was a great beating of wings, and another Cthulu appeared. It dived, almost taking them in its sudden plunge. Above, it circled, eyes hungry, desperate for meat. This one was bigger. It opened its mouth and let out an eerie howl, making them all wince in pain as an orchestra of a hundred mistuned violins screeched together. It was like nails being dragged across a blackboard. The beast turned again, and lunged. They ducked, plunging into the snow, and it missed by inches. Shea could almost feel the scales of the great beast scraping her head as it passed overhead.

They had to charm it. In the middle of the confusion, Alex ducked, holding the pendant in the light. The great scaly monster swerved and pulled up, as the sharp beam hit its retina.

"Make it crash!" Anya was yelling "Make it crash! We can get on it!"

Trying desperately, Alex swung the pendant in the light. The monsters were going crazy, veering and swerving, keeping their distance from the powerful ray. A gut-wrenching noise issued from their beaked mouths, and their eyes widened. To their left, one swung in, beating its great bat-like wings, eager for food.

Oh God, thought Anya.

She was on her knees in the snow. She watched, petrified, as the great beast swooped towards them. Alex turned, catching it full beam. The monster's head flew to one side, its eyes screwed up in clear agony. But it wasn't watching its flight path. Alex threw himself out of its way, as the scaly underbelly hit the cold snow-covered floor.

There were more. As Anya glanced behind, a hundred streamed towards them. "Duck!" she cried, just in time, as yet another scaly underbelly passed over their heads. Eyes streaming, she looked up. The thing was in mid-air, hovering like a giant crow. It looked at her with great yellow eyes, and plunged.

On the ground, their Cthulu lurched sideways, violently in the snow. Anya ran and dug her nails into the hide, desperate for something more to grip, swinging a leg over its spine, praying. Behind her the others ran, Alex abandoning hope and flailing the pendant in an arch round his head as the great beasts beat their wings. Their Cthulu screeched as Alex reached it, the shiny pendant in his hand burning its eyes. They struggled on, pulling themselves over the bony spine, digging their nails tightly into scaly flesh.

"GO!" cried Anya "GO! GO! GO!"

Whether the Cthulu understood or not, or whether the pendant had disappeared from its range of sight as Alex had clambered on, she didn't know. Two great wings fanned out, and they shot into the air with a sudden jolt. The ride was lumpy and Anya thought she was going to be sick. In front of her Alex swung the pendant, trying to control their direction, but it only served to make the Cthulu scream loudly, and lurch in-mid air, its members following.

Clinging on, Anya just had time to see knife-long talons dangling in front of her face before it happened. The pain that shot through her shoulder was unbelievable. White hot wire was pressing to her skin, making her scream. Hot blood was pouring from her: she could feel its warmth, yet she couldn't keep the feeling in her arm. It was going numb. She felt sick, blinded by pain. Her vision was slipping.

"Hold on!" shouted Shea. "Don't let go!"

At the front, Alex knew there was something wrong. The vile and rusty smell of blood entered his senses, making him twist round. Anya's face was pale, eyed wide in fear and shock. Behind that was Shea, her brown hair whipped back from her likewise pale face. He couldn't see Charlie, but he guessed he was there somewhere, his ginger hair likewise ripped back, exposing him to the cold blasts as the grim monsters swept past.

He turned back. Before him was a Cthulu, hurtling towards them. Alex could see the round, yellow eyes. He pulled, and their monster reared. They were vertical in the air, each member clinging on with their nails, legs dangling, bashing the person below. Anya couldn't see; the pain in her arm was horrific. Any minute now she'd have to let go. Her boots hit Shea, knocking against her shoulders. Her hands had gone white. Her shoulder felt like it was swelling. From below she heard an echoey screech, and knew the others were not far behind.

Their beast lunched forwards, and Shea found herself almost parallel, head pressed against Anya's back. She dug in her nails, not daring to reposition her shaking hands, and tried to grip with her legs, but it was no good. Again they dived, and Anya slid forwards, hitting Alex in the back as he tried to control the rearing monster.

Another screech.

Behind her, Shea ducked. Their monster lunged again, its whole body snaking back and forth like a giant anaconda in flight. She screamed openly as red hot air whistled past her, burning her ears. They were going to die. This was a stupid, hair-brained experiment and they were all going to die! Behind, Charlie was clinging on tightly, his knuckles white as he gripped the creature's scaly hide. The monster reared, and Alex was lifted from his seat. At the rear, Charlie clung on for dear life. Time was passing unbelievably quickly; Shea couldn't keep track of which beast was where, and hoped Alex was having better luck. Again, an earth-shattering screech sounded in her ears, as though it was right alongside her. She closed her eyes, praying silently.

Please God, let this be over.

Her heart pounded restlessly in her chest, making her feel sick and dizzy as adrenaline kept her white knuckled clamped around the creature's scaly hide. She could feel her body turning in all the different ways as their Cthulu swerved and dodged the fire-breathing fiends. There was a sudden jolt. Shea thought they must either have been swallowed whole, or else had had crashed into the side of the mountain. She waited, expecting the pitching feeling of a fall, or a screaming pain as she was ripped limb from limb.

Nothing came. Neither of those two senses entered her thoughts. She had no idea where she was, nor where the others were. She grimaced, shaking, not yet daring to open her eyes. From behind she felt a nudge. No, she could not be alone. Something else was moving too.

She opened her eyes. Some way beneath her, Charlie was flat out in the snow. He appeared to have fallen off. Shea was about to cry out, then realised that she too, could not be far from the ground. Charlie, at least, looked very life-sized lying there, his ginger hair swept back from his pale forehead.

Her fringe brushed something cold. In front of her, Anya was sitting, not moving one bit. Shea supposed she must be shaken too, exhausted by their whirl-wind adventure.

She opened a hand, releasing it from scaly hide. It was painful, having gripped the Cthulu tight in fear. Shea flexed the sore digits. They were white-matching the snow around them. Slowly, she extended on, pale, shaking, finger, and poked Anya in the back. She didn't move. Shea poked her again, this time somewhat harder, and the girl stirred a little.

There was a sudden thud, and Shea looked up. Below her, Alex's eyes were round, mystified they had made it across alive. He must have just dismounted. In front, Anya began to shake. Shea strongly suspected she was crying, tears of joy or relief. She would have done so herself, had she the energy, but she felt exhausted. Certainly she felt tired for having done nothing but cower for the past thirty minutes.

In the snow, Charlie stirred. He seemed to be coming out of a deep sleep, for he began to groan and move his limbs slowly about on the white carpet. Something was wrong. Shea unhooked her leg and slid off, amazed at how much it ached, down the brown scaly back, landing with a thud at his side. She felt dazed, but leant over him.

"Are you alright?" she asked.

Charlie groaned and closed his eyes. Shea suspected that he had never much been one for heights. A sudden rush of faintness came over her and she swayed, stumbling at Charlie's head as she tried to maintain her balance. Someone came striding over.

"You alright?" a voice asked. Shea nodded and smiled weakly, and from behind them there was a racking sob as Anya appeared to come to life. Alex gave her a small half smile, and disappeared, supposedly to help dismount their friend.

She sat down. Coldness hit her like an arctic truck. Still, it was better than fainting. Actually, lying down might be best.

Shea lowered herself to the cold ground and closed her eyes against the dazzling whiteness. A slight breeze ruffled her fringe. She opened her eyes momentarily, to see Alex helping a very slow and trembling Anya across an icy patch, three feet away. Again she closed her eyes. Bliss. She was alive! Relief and peace swept over her like it was contained in the very breeze. Close by, Charlie groaned and twitched, but nothing more.

When Shea next opened her eyes, she found herself staring into two very blue pupils.

"Alright?" asked a voice from nearby.

Shea tried to sit up, and a great dizziness swept over her again, making the world spin. She gulped down air and nodded. Yeah, she was okay, just as long as they never had to do that again. Slowly, she turned her head. Charlie was still lying there, his knees slightly curled into his body. He appeared to be sound asleep; in any case he made no noise and did not seem to be responding to Alex's voice. Alex bent over him, then looked back at Shea.

"I think we'd best leave him for a bit." he told her. "Here."

He handed her a blue cup of steaming liquid, turning back to Charlie. She took it, gulping it gratefully. A heated glow surged through her windpipe, warming her, and she felt instantly better.

"Thanks." she gasped.

Alex was still examining Charlie. Frowning, he dropped his backpack, and began rummaging inside, bringing out a coloured sheet, which he spread over the unmoved body. Then he left, going to Anya, appearing to kneel down and ask her some questions. Anya, at least, appeared to be awake, if slightly tearful, for her replies seem to come in great sobbing breaths. Shea saw Alex pass her the cup, and relived the warm surge through her body, knowing Anya would soon feel it too.

She lay back down and curled up, knowing that lying on snow was potentially bad for her, but not caring much. Soon she felt something being draped over her, and knew Alex was there. Still, she kept her eyes shut. She was too tired to even thank him.

She must have drifted into sleep. Again she was soaring over a vast green lake, it's emerald surface lapping coldly like the giant eye of a monster. There were screeches in the air, and Shea turned to find herself face to face with at least seven Cthulus. They seemed livid; hot on her tail. She pulled the red reigns attached to her Cthulu's neck, when all of a sudden the great beast lurched and dived. Emerald green water rose up to meet her. She closed her eyes, fearing the worst . . .

Shea awoke with a shudder, and opened her eyes. All around her, the snow was white. She wondered if they'd moved yet. She was feeling slightly confused-if they had plunged into the lake, then why was she here, lying on ground that felt mildly warm despite the fact she should probably be freezing? She moved her head, and caught a disorientating vision of a pair of brown boots and thighs. Shuffling, she tried to get a better look, and realised with a start that it was Alex, or someone who looked remarkably like Alex, upside down. But he couldn't be upside down; that made no sense! Shea blinked and turned her head, and another image of Alex swarmed into her vision. This time, he was the right way up. Still dressed in arctic clothing, he seemed to be attending to some sort of bonfire.

Shea sat up. Rubbing her eyes, she peered out of them like they were dusty windows. No, Alex was still there. He was real.

"Alex!" she called out, and her voice seemed to break as she cried his name. Across the snow, the boy looked up, offering her a lopsided grin that barely concealed his relief. He got up and walked over to her, sitting down, and again offered her a drink. The potion streamed before her in it's blue cup.

"What's this?" asked Shea, for the second time.

"Just drink it."

Shea did as she was told, finishing the goblet in two almighty gulps. She had not realised how thirsty she was.

"What . . . what is it?" she asked again, hoping it was something good. It certainly felt good. The liquid seemed to flow through her insides, bringing her a warmth she could barely remember feeling. She waggled her fingers and toes and looked up, expecting to see him towering over her. But Alex had already walked away.

"Hey!" cried Shea getting up. She felt instantly restored. "What's in that? It's like magic!"

She stood and walked to the campfire, surprised at how easy this was, and felt it's warm glow touch her cold gloved fingers. Alex was sitting down, and Shea plonked herself besides him. He was roasting something on a stick, holding it out to the orange flames.

"What's that?" she asked.

"Rat."

"No, seriously, what is it?"

"Rat."

"What?!"

"They do exist out here, y'know."

"Rats?"

"Yeah, rats."

"Okay . . . well, where did you get them from?"

"Out here."

"Oh come on, Alex!" Shea tipped her head to the side. "Rats? Out here? I don't think so!"

"It's true!" Alex turned the spit–roast rats on their spike, and drew it back from the flames. Shea could see several little brown bodies, skewered on the end.

"That's disgusting!"

"It's food. Here-" Alex slid one off the end and held it out for her. "Try it."

Shea drew back, folding her arms in disgust. "No way!"

"Go on!" Alex shrugged, and bit ferociously into one. "S'good. Anyway, tastes like chicken."

"Yuck!"

Shea pulled a face, but Alex merely slid another off the spike, and gave it to her. He nodded, as she held it unwillingly up to her mouth. Slowly, she closed her eyes and took a bite. It was surprisingly hot, warm to a tongue that hadn't touched food in over four hours. And it did taste like chicken.

"Mmm . . ." she nodded in surprise. "S'goood!"

There was a groan from behind them, and they both turned to see Charlie stir. Alex stood up and took the cup to him, and Shea watched as Charlie gulped down the amazing liquor. In time Charlie edged close to them, and soon it was only Anya who was left to wake. Alex decided to rouse her; probably a good idea, as the rats were getting cold. She awoke, bleary eyed and confused, but was soon munching quietly at their side in a pensive sort of way. She appeared shaken by their ordeal, and Shea noticed a red bandage across one arm.

Presently it began to grow colder, and the group began to shiver. Alex stood up. None of them wanted to move, but he insisted they should go on, before the night closed in around them, and they became frozen.

They moved slowly about in the cold, arms numb. Walking was slow. Time seemed to slow and stop. Around them the light gradually faded, claiming the whiteness back for its own. They had to find shelter.

"I see it!" called Anya, after an hour's blinding run. Her arm was aching and she could not think of anything else. Standing about a hundred feet away, in the swirling whiteness, stood a giant cave. The cavernous mouth lay open, playing host, inviting them in from the smarting cold.

They trooped inside. It wasn't warm, but at least it would be dry compared to the weather outside. Together, they groaned a sigh of relief. They were used to Anya being right. She may have been a bit shaky, but as a journalist she had strong eyes, always on the lookout for things. It was a respite they desperately needed. Settling down, they warmed their glucose drinks and gulped them greedily down. Anya's bandage was changed for her by Alex. The gash wasn't deep, thank God-it would certainly heal in time-but Alex, thinking of what he, himself, could do to others, shuddered to think what they might yet have to face. Together they repacked, and settling down, told stories, until Anya decided it was time for them all to go to bed, ready for the last haul tomorrow.

THE CASTLE

THEY'D FINALLY TREKKED on. In the four hours of bitingly cold wind, a grey shape had loomed before them like a beacon of hope. Charlie couldn't tell if he was hallucinating or not. The icy wind bit at his cheeks, despite pulling his hood over his head and donning his snow goggles. Finally it seemed the blob wasn't just in his mind. It was a castle.

The castle lay in icy mists before them-a ruin of a place, stone walls tumbling around it. Windswept and lost, the crew gazed fearfully down upon the scene that lay before them. The mist rose in an icy whirlwind, picking up speed. All around grew the feeling of anxiety, caused by the presence of the dangers that lay before them. Fear swept their very souls as though the ominous castle had sent ghosts before them, ready to turn them away, and send them scuttling in haste back over the mountain tops. But Shea wasn't ready to give in that easily. All around, the storm grew denser, a hurricane of noise, snatching with icy fingers at their clothes, making each heartbeat louder.

By the time they had reached it, everyone was freezing. Anya huddled closer as they stood, wind-swept and forlorn in the biting cold. Stood at the bottom, they looked like nothing more than lost sheep, huddling in the cold, desperate for shelter. Above, the castle's cold stone walls bore down on them as they stared at the greying mass that rose like an icy pinnacle, lording over them. High, high above stood the top tower. It was something from a fairy tale.

Anya shivered. It had been a right haul even across the last leg of the trek. Now they were supposed to somehow get inside this thing. She looked across at the rest of the group, who seemed to be thinking exactly the same. Shea had whipped out her laptop.

"Yup." she called. "He's inside there."

No-one responded. Now they had got there, Anya wondered just how prepared they were to take on this mysterious Mr X. She wasn't. Her heart quaked at such a thought.

"Any ways in?" asked Charlie.

Shea surveyed the screen, and looked up at the greying towers that stood ominously before them.

"Err . . . well," she called across the swirling drifts, "according to this tracker, look; it's quite a complex place. Mr X is here, see. This dot, just here. So we have to avoid him."

Charlie peered over her shoulder.

"Who's gonna to take on Mr X?" he voiced.

No-one moved. No-one even stirred. Anya could tell from their faces that each was holding their breath, not willing to be the first to speak.

"I mean . . . how . . . how do we, y'know, kill this guy?" asked Charlie "Do we run him through, or what?"

Shea thought hard. How *did* you kill a demon?

"By stabbing him with the dagger." Anya replied. Even her jaw chattered in the biting breeze.

"That he's got?"

"Err . . . well, yeah."

It was a grim prospect. No-one actually really wanted to meet the notorious man now they had finally got there. Shea gulped in the cold air. Yeah. She wasn't looking forward to murdering someone, but if that's what it took, well, then so be it.

"So," she began, trying to move the awkward silence that seemed to be pressing in on them. "We'll, well; we can get in through any window, seeing as they have no glass, though probably not the one at the top of the tower-"

Alex looked up. *No joke*, he thought.

"-or we can get in through here, here or here. Personally I don't think it ideal for us to go in together, just in case, y'know, we get attacked or one of us is captured, or something-"

Captured? Alex thought. He'd better not be captured. The prospect of coming out alive from any place that contained Red Caps, he knew, was extremely thin to none. Was she mad? Was *he* mad? Now they'd got there, he wasn't quite sure.

"-so I think it'd be ideal if we split into two groups. Alex and I will take this window, and Anya and Charlie, you can take that one."

Right. Well. That settled it.

"Okay? So, we'll . . . we'll leave it like that then, and, yeah, if we leave our bags here, cos it'll make us quieter, see?"

Everybody dropped their bags. There was definitely a note of defeat in the thuds that sounded as they hit the snowy ground.

They split up into their respective groups. Once Mr X saw, and threatened Anya, Charlie would rush in, distracting him, giving Alex or Shea time to grab the dagger. That way they would know where it was, if it was on him. Which it might not be. And in that case they'd all better scarper. Fast.

Anya wasn't very happy with the plan. She read and wrote about people's tragedies every day, but she wasn't one for being part of them. The fact that none of them knew what lay inside, didn't exactly help. Suppose there were Red Caps just waiting? Still, that was the plan. And, since she couldn't think of any other, Anya decided she might as well go with it. None of them could. Added to that, what she would do if Shea or any of the others was hurt or captured she didn't know. Swallowing hurriedly, she flung the dreaded thought from her mind, and tried to focus on the task ahead.

Scaling the wall wasn't easy. They may have climbed mountains to get there, but at least they were something you could drive your pick into. Here there was nothing-the stone walls lay cold and flat, and her boots scraped in a futile effort against them. In the end, Charlie outstripped her, and had to haul her up onto the window ledge.

Yeah. Great. Very 'knight in shining armour'.

Anya couldn't but help feel a little bit stupid as she rolled over the ledge and touched down on the stone slabs below, her boots creating a ringing sound across what appeared to be a chamber, as they hit the icy floor. It was round, almost a perfect circle, the white stone slabs rising to an icy point above. Across from them lay a heavy wooden door, looking almost fortified in its appearance. Great. It was probably locked. Together they crossed the floor, and, preparing themselves for any attack, lest their footfalls be heard, Anya twisted the grey iron bar.

The door swung open with surprising ease. Even more surprising was that nothing flew at them-no demons, no bats or minarets; nothing. Anya felt almost disappointed—what was the point in hyping yourself up if these things weren't going to happen?

On the other side of the door, they found themselves at the top of an equally cold looming staircase, chiselled broken-handedly from great slate slabs, and, proceeding down it with bated breath, found themselves in front of another large oak door. This too, was unlocked. Did Mr. X have no sense of security? Or was this a false trap, intentionally leading them to believe their task would be easy, tricking them to gullibility? Anya tightened her grip on her weapon-her pick-and swung it aside, to reveal only a wide stone corridor, leading to yet another door, another chamber, another staircase. Again there was another corridor. This really was a sense of déjà-vu. Was it that they were simply going around in circles? Yet they couldn't be, she was sure. The temperature dropped by degrees as the minutes ticked. She hoped the others, behind them, had not found Mr. X. No way were they ready for a distraction.

Yet another corridor. This was crazy. Behind her, Charlie's breath rose in icy mists in the otherwise deserted passageway.

Down and down they went. Down and down. Then a door, the last door, she was certain.

She pushed it aside. There stood a grim man, tall with a bald head, dressed in what appeared to be leathers. Slowly he turned his head, and two eyes locked upon hers, making the breath freeze in her throat. At least, she assumed it was two eyes. She couldn't really tell, because of the glasses he appeared to be wearing. Black glasses. What struck her the most, though, was not that this character seemed to be dressed, from head to toe, in black, nor even the glasses, but his face. It seemed to be covered in dye. A huge tattoo of a broken sun ran coldly down his forehead to his cheeks, racing right across his bony nose to the very bottom of his chin. It was something from a nightmare. What on earth did it mean?

The man raised one long arm, pointing his bony pale fingers at her.

"*Intruder!*" spat a cold, high voice, one she did not expect to come from a man so big. "*Kill them!*"

At once a thousand Red Caps sped across the room towards her. She did not have time to respond. Anya closed her eyes and prayed. She could feel their grip tight on her shoulders, and when she opened them again was not surprised to see she was held several feet off the floor. Close by she could hear Charlie gasp-it sounded like he was being strangled. She tried to turn her head, but the armour clad hand tightened around her throat, restricting her breathing.

"*Where are they?*" came the cruel high voice from below.

"Don't know what you-" Charlie's voice broke off in a sudden gasp. It seemed the hand around his throat had just tightened.

"*Let the girl speak.*" came the voice. It had the horrid ring of authority, of enjoyment, as if whoever it was, was enjoying some sort of sick show, "*Ladies first . . .*"

Anya didn't know what to say. If there was one thing she was certain of, it was that she would not give away the other's presence, no matter what it took. She was resolutely set against it.

"*Where are they?*" came the voice again.

"Who?" asked Anya, as best she could against the strong arm that gripped her throat.

Below, there was a sudden echo of cold, manic laughter. Good God! thought Anya. The man was clearly more than dangerous; he was a bloody psychopath! Her heart beat against her ribs in a fight or flight pattern-lub dub, lub dub, lub dub! But she wouldn't let him know she was scared.

"*Where are the others?*" came the voice, almost mocking now, "*The other two? Where are they hiding? Don't make me hurt you now . . .*"

Anya was near enough shaking. She hated to think what he meant by 'hurt her'. Whatever it was, it couldn't be good. Beside her, Charlie's breath came in short sharp gasps. He was evidently in deep trouble.

"I'm sorry," called Anya, "but it's only us. Just us two. No more."

"*Liar*!" the voice seethed, and Anya could almost hear the wrath in it. "*Tell me! Tell me! Where are they?!*"

The hand that gripped Anya shook her in mid air. She swung helplessly to and fro, like the pendulum of a clock. Whatever was happening to her couldn't be near as bad as it was for Charlie. As she swung she realised she could no longer hear his gasps. Perhaps he had fainted. With desperate thoughts she hoped so-death by suffocation was not deemed pleasant. She wondered where on earth Shea and Alex were right now. Perhaps they might be close by. If the worst came to the worst, they had already been captured, and her lying to Mr X would only result in a more serious death. The prospect was frightening enough already, but Anya didn't want it to be any more painful than it already would be. The thought of death made her mind spin, as she gasped for air. Her vision was beginning to go funny, and a dull ache had begun in the forefront of her mind. *Must think!* thought Anya, as her ribs rose and fell in shallow breaths, as their capacity decreased. Oxygen starvation. She felt exactly like a fish out of water, trying to draw in non-existent air that she could not filter. She felt sick and weak. Her limbs moved restlessly as she attempted to loosen the grip around her neck, but it was too strong. Again came the laughter, higher and more manic than before. Black patches were beginning to appear before her, obscuring her already blurred vision. She thought she was ready to pass out.

Just as she was ready to give up, and succumb to the weight that pressed down on her, there was a sudden, deafening crack, and what sounded like a large aeroplane landed beneath her feet. Then, there was a scream, high pitched with fear. Darkness consumed her, and she blacked out.

Running The Maze

ALEX WAS CONFUSED. Left in a spiralling maze, Shea had run off so quickly he had no idea where she had gone. The room before him was a maze of passageways. It was hexagonal, like a giant tomb or secret cavern. There were three entrances, all on the same side, archways close together. *Which one had she gone through?* Alex wondered, trying to remember. It was crucial; if she'd gone through the one he didn't choose, they could end up miles apart, just from the angles. He tried to think. She'd seen *something*. His mind played and replayed the scene but he couldn't remember: all he could see was a black, cloaked *thing*. Well, he supposed it *was* a thing; it had to be *some*thing after all; black things didn't miraculously disappear, and he didn't think Shea would have gone so quickly if there was nothing important there.

He chose a path, hoping it was right, and began walking, trying to convince himself, but it grew darker as he tunnelled further. The floor seemed to be sloping, leading him downwards, then it flattened, and tilted up. Alex was almost in pitch blackness, hands scraping the wall, feeling his way. He could hear a muffled rumbling sound and turned his head, trying to distinguish where the noise was coming from, or what it was. It sounded like a motor, or cars on a distant road, but it was coming closer, getting louder. Alex climbed further, suddenly hopeful, glad he was not the only one in the passage. It might be one of the others. Then the noise drew away. Alex stopped and craned to listen. It was a faint hum now . . . almost . . . . no, nothing. Silence descended. He walked on, shuffling through the darkness. Beneath his foot, something creaked, and Alex paused. He leant forwards. There it was, beneath his shoe; a creaking sound. Perhaps it was a trap. Unsure how long it went for, Alex wondered if he could jump it. He stuck his leg out a little further, testing his weight. In the darkness, the floor groaned. Keeping his weight on one sole, Alex leant across, and his toe touched the ground. No, that was as far as he could go.

Alex wondered what he should do. Retreat? Would he be able to find the same room? He didn't think he'd passed anything that would give him difficulty; he certainly hadn't changed tracks, not that he knew of anyway. Maybe he would just have to risk it. If the others were still separated, perhaps the Red Caps had found them by now. He had to get there. He turned several paces back, and ran, leaping high into the air. For a few seconds he knew what it must be like to be a pilot; absolutely weightless. It was lasting forever; surely he'd made it. Then it was touchdown.

Alex heard something break. Darkness swallowed him, as the passageway completely, and utterly, disappeared.

A Two
Legged Race

S HEA, COMING TO a stop, turned around to find Alex was not behind her. In the darkened passageway, she turned to her tracker, realising Mr X had now, truly outwitted her.

On the screen, dots were moving. They were far away; heading to the outside of the screen. It was unfortunate the tracker didn't also show the routes of the passageways she was in. But it was modern; an up-to-date little gizmo relying on satellite technology. Shea doubted that there were even such things as satellites when this ruin was built. On the screen, something was moving; swarms of red things. An icon popped up . . . Red Caps.

Shea stared at the screen, then looked wildly behind her, spinning around as if expecting to be swarmed upon at any minute. This was the first time she would ever come face to face with them. They were deadly. She'd seen the photos of the teenagers, of course, eyes closed, clothes stained with crusts of dried blood. For some reason she'd never thought they were real. Now she'd seen them, everything had come to light; seen the real reason why they had trekked so many miles in arctic cold to reach frozen stone ruins. From the encounter she'd had, Shea wasn't sure she wanted another. Still, she wasn't exactly in a position to back out now. Knowing she had to move, she sprinted on, further into the disorientating abyss, heart pounding. The maze had got darker and her breath caught in her throat. She gasped, trying to calm herself. Alex could not be far. Perhaps she should go back the way she came. Cursing, Shea took the left, half-running in the dark, knowing she had probably taken the wrong route. There was something at the end—a door-she could see it now, growing into view as the darkness came to the end. On her wrist, the dark specks raced forwards. They'd be upon her in minutes. The door would act as a barrier-she had to take it, now, before they reached her.

Shea pulled open the door, and swung it shut behind her. She turned. Before her stood a horrific sight. Two Red Caps were stood, side by side, holding what appeared to be two lifeless human forms. Then she realised. It was Anya and Charlie, pale and ghostly, skin white against auburn hair. On the opposite side stood what appeared to be a mannequin. A horrible sun tattoo stretched across its skin like a giant burn mark.

Mr X. He was quite as horrible as she had seen in Anya's book-although not tall, there was something about him that made her blood run cold. He stared sickeningly at her, like a wolf eying its prey, and yet she remained, frozen, unable to tear away from those blood red eyes.

Then he opened his mouth. It was like nothing she'd ever heard before; high and cold and chilling to the core. She felt a burning in the small of her back, and fell head-first towards the floor. Shea knew instantly she'd been tasered; her spine had locked and, face down and vulnerable, her limbs refused to move. Cursing internally, there was nothing she could do.

Something snatched at her, and she suddenly found herself dangling high in the air. A vice like limb gripped her feet, making her want to scream in pain as she felt her bones cracking. She dangled helplessly, realising she was in deep trouble, no longer in a position to fight or save. She could feel the blood slide down her body. A pain had started in her forehead, making her feel sick. She tried to think. Her headache was getting worse, making her want to gag, but her throat was locked tight and her chest contracted painfully, forcing her to breathe in short, painful gasps. The pressure was now immense, threatening her thoughts. Circles of purple appeared before her eyes. Shea felt like some one was squeezing her head. She blinked, and the room swam in and out of focus. No longer could she see him. An empty, echoing sound was bouncing in her brain, filling her ears. Her eyes felt heavy and she felt herself slipping into sleep. She tried to fight it, feeling the energy drain from her limbs, holding it off, hoping that somehow, Alex would realise the danger they were in.

THROUGH THE
TRAPDOOR

ALEX COULD FEEL himself falling. Darkness surrounded him and his torso twisted frantically in mid air. His legs flailed and his boots scuffed stone. He put out his arms, trying to break his fall, and they snapped upwards as his lower limbs plummeted beneath him. Further he was falling, further and further. His feet made painful contact, and he crumpled forwards. An unknown force rose out of the pitch to strike his forehead, and he blacked out.

When he woke, Alex couldn't figure out why. Something was lapping his face. It felt like the rough tongue of a dog. But it was too cold, and too wet. Then he realised: water.

He rolled over and suddenly felt drenched as a sudden icy chill seeped into his clothes. He sat up. Dizziness overcame him, forcing him to almost faint. A sickening pain came sharp to the front, and Alex tried to remember what had happened. He had fallen, so this must be . . . he stood up, and the pain became worse, banging around his head like a kettle drum. He bent over, trying to keep as low as possible, screwing up his eyes, trying to concentrate on the yellow sunspots that danced beneath his eyelids. He felt sick. A banging echoed in his ears: louder, like a heartbeat. He tried to steady himself, breathing hard, breathless, telling himself the pain would pass. From somewhere came the sound of gushing. A coldness touched his socks, and Alex opened his eyes to find himself now ankle deep in water. Pain shot through him, and he closed them again. It was coming in. The coldness was now seeping up his calves like climbing ivy. Alex shivered and tried to think. If it was coming in . . . the only way he knew of how to come in was from above. He felt panic rising in his chest and forced himself to swallow it. Now was not the time to panic. He straightened up, took a breath, and opened his eyes, throwing his head upwards. Above, a shadowy outline of the ceiling greeted him. Alex breathed heavily, trying to regain his balance. The grey box above told him that his entrance was still open. Forcing himself not to shut his eyes, he glared past the blue dots of pain, glancing for the source. There! Water was pouring in like anything. Alex waded up the hole and placed his hand over, but the force was too great, and the pressure left rivulets running beneath his palm.

The only is up, thought Alex. Well, there was one plan. It wasn't entirely foolproof, but the laws of common sense told Alex that if you could get in one way, you must be able to get out. And, as there was only one possible opening, he would have to use his resources. Alex knew the human body could float-and in that knowledge lay his plan. If he could float up to that hole, the water would take him all the way, and he would have to swim out of the cave. Which way would he be facing, though, once he reached the corridor? That was, of course, if he made it up in the first place. Still, the water was now knee high, and Alex, forgetting not to panic, was in no state of mind to think of another plan. The water reached his thighs, reached his hips-Alex gasped as the coldness closed around him, making his arms and legs numb. Breathing deeply so as to remain calm, he waited until it had almost reached his neck before he began to tread water. Still it poured. Alex couldn't hear it now; the opening was underwater, and though he couldn't see it, he knew he was shaking. The room was filling up-soon there would be more below than above him.

He didn't have to wait long. Up and up he went, floating breathlessly, watching as each brick was swallowed and drowned. The coldness was stealing his breath, freezing his ribcage, making it difficult to breathe. Then came the ceiling; bearing down upon him. Alex lined himself up with the shaft. This was his only chance. Below, the icy water rolled, lapping up the walls, reaching to lick the ceiling with an icy tongue. It was a foot away. Alex panted, struggling in the enclosed box. If he got stuck now . . . he pushed upwards, his hands brushing the stone walls. Alex glanced skywards, hoping to see light through the shaft, but all was black. There was a barrier.

They must have shut off the tunnel.

A cold feeling of dread closed over his heart. He was going to die. He twisted around. Coldness swept across his shoulders. The water was still rising. It would engulf him. This couldn't be it! There had to be another way! The water carried him upwards, towards doom. Alex's hand shot out, and he struck something that was defiantly not stone: wood.

The floor!

He punched, lashing out, and his hand struck it again. He twisted, bashing it, willing it to break. The water was still rising. Alex's hand made contact, and the wood splintered. Losing no time, Alex took one, deep breath, as the biting numbness swept over his mouth and nose, and plunged upwards in the icy water, hands scrabbling. They made contact with the ledge and he hauled himself up, propelling himself into the corridor once more, forwards, twisting away from the source of water that gushed in behind him.

Fresh air. He gasped in the cold sweetness. Water was still rising. The corridor would be swamped before long. He stumbled along in the black, heavy clothing bearing him down. Which way was it? The water was knee-high now; thigh-deep, still rising. Within seconds it stole over his torso, lifting his feet, bearing him aloft. He trod water, gulping in the last lungfuls of air. When it reached the ceiling he would have no-where to go but out. Now it was at his shoulders, now his neck. He held his breath. Heart beating in his ears, he could not see the passage in front of him. Nor did he know how long it went on for, or if it even had an end. Alex tried thinking logically, knowing panicking would only use the air in his lungs: something he desperately needed to hold on to. Darkness danced around him, as it rose over his eyes, sealing the blackness, and he felt the cold dullness lift his fringe. There was nowhere but forward.

His muscles ached as he scrabbled, using the wall of the passageway, meandering like a crab. He reached out, his hand brushing cold stone, leading him like the blind. His feet bobbed, pushing down, trailing along the bottom. He felt he was moon-walking. There was another, and another. He had to go forward. He stretched out a thigh, pushed on the next stone, and felt it crack. Before he could think even a single thought, Alex slipped through the darkness, hurtling once more to the floor below.

He hit it hard, hands over his head. Shockwaves reverberated around him as water poured itself upon him, drenching his already sodden form. Struggling, Alex held his hands to his eyes, trying to stop the sting, and staggered to his feet, trying to roll himself away from the onpouring mass. Behind, water gushed in. Alex wiped his hands away, and looked around, blinking rapidly under sodden eyelashes. In the corner stood a giant oak door. Panting, astounded to be alive, he staggered straight towards it, shutting and sealing it, leaving the drowning tide behind.

He limped out into the empty passageway. He could not be far. To his left stood a large, fortified door. From somewhere nearby he could hear noises, like talking. He turned the handle, and pushed it open. And a truly horrific sight met his eyes.

A World Of Evil

THE NEXT THING that happened was not good. Shea lay, face down, on the cold stone floor, her mind desperately wandering, screaming out in pain. There was a thud behind her, and the strong arm lifted her back into the air, high above its face. A disgusting green creature looked at her through pale yellow eyes. A foul stench reached her, as it breathed out against her face in a snort of blue smoke. It was horrific. Shea's forehead screamed out against her torture. The demon dropped her again, slamming her to near unconsciousness.

Stowing her carelessly under its arm, the creature began to move. Shea swung helplessly, still not in control of her own body. Ahead a grey wall came up to face her. Surely they weren't going to go through it? But the demon seemed to have no need for solid structures. Shea closed her eyes, waiting for the head on collision, but nothing came. Instead she felt only a brief gust-like they had entered a tunnel, and when she opened her eyes it was back on the other side of the wall. Something blue dripped to the floor in an stringy stream. Saliva. Obviously it was eying her up. Looked like she was next for dinner.

Suddenly something changed. She felt the Red Cap stiffen, and the hanging stream dropped. The Red Cap moved forwards. It lolloped, almost benignly, down the corridor and turned, opening the large hinged door, and took her back inside.

Inside, the room was not immediately different to the corridor. Then came a voice. A voice of menace. It did not sound good. Shea realised instantly they had just returned to the previous room; the same room where Anya and Charlie remained trussed up like turkeys, held as captives against two more giant beasts.

The man was now stood in the middle of the room. He was tall, gaunt, human-like. The long tattoo was spread across his brow and face, concealing most of his features; the tall pointed nose, the thin lips curled into a cruel smile, the eyes covered with black shades.

There was a thud behind them. Evidently the door had closed. Well, he had three out of four.

There was a bang as the door flew open again. Out of the corner of her eye, Shea could see something green and red. To her right, Anya seemed to have passed out, lifted weightlessly from the floor. Charlie too, seemed to be still struggling, his face red as his supply of oxygen began to run out. The creature was suffocating him. Not that it seemed to mind at all.

A dull thud, a sudden intake of breath, and she knew at once who had entered. Shea thought of trying to twist round to see him, but her lungs felt compressed, and didn't think she could fight the weight of muscle that was lifting her, one handed, from the floor.

The man was laughing; high, cruel, cold. There was another thud, another intake of breath. Shea lifted up her chin, trying to breathe some air, but the arm across her chest only tightened and she found herself like a gormless fish, strung high and dry. The air was clogging up before her, and a vile smell of burning hair reached her nostrils. Her eyes were watering with what appeared to be thick, green fog. The laughter pounded against her earlobes, jarring up her brain. Then, all was quiet, as she slipped away . . .

ALEX ARRIVES

ALEX GASPED. HE felt like had just been punched twice in the stomach. Nearby, Shea, Charlie and Anya were being held high by three green monsters, legs dangling in mid-air. In the middle of the room, a man was talking. He was tall, dressed in a long black robe. His eyes, covered by shades, were surveying Alex, and he was smiling coldly. A large black image of a sun was stretched across his face, like he had gone overboard with a marker pen. It was vile. The temperature in the room suddenly dropped, as though he'd walked into a freezer, and Alex's blood ran cold with fear. He didn't have to ask who it was. This was not what they'd planned. He had no idea how they'd ended up captured so quickly. How could their plan have gone *so* wrong?

In front of him, the man was talking. He was hissing and spitting, glaring at him with those awful shaded eyes, like this was normal, like he expected Alex to understand. Alex had no idea what the man was trying to say; he didn't seem to speak English, and Alex wasn't entirely sure he wasn't having a fit. A lot of words were leaving his lips, contorting the air, rupturing his ears; words he had never heard in any tongue. Alex stared around as the words bounced off the walls, magnifying them ten-fold. At the far end of the cave was a faint white glow, just beyond his range of vision. He took a glance across, trying to think, and at once wished he hadn't. Bile rose to his throat, and he swallowed hard.

They were skeletons, hanging up, with chains shackling their wrists, binding them tight against the cold stone wall. Broken bones, white and brittle, littered the backdrop-remnants of unfortunate victims. Alex could see the way the splintered shafts had rotted and bleached. How long had he held them here? Some must have been newer: chunks of hair and decomposing flesh clinging to the rotting corpses. The stench was terrible: he could almost taste the acrid flesh on his tongue. He had never come across a sight so sickeningly gruesome. The man, with his back to them, could not see them. And then . . . Fear once again came over him, sickeningly; suddenly startling. At the end of the cave, in amidst the mangled corpses, something moved. Alex squinted. Someone was there. Standing with its back to the wall, held up like a puppet . . . but it *couldn't* be . . .

Then it's head turned, and Alex almost fainted.

It was a girl. A young girl; dressed in torn garments, her wild hair dimly strewn across her face. Alex took one look at her scarred, broken body, and anger rose in him like a coursing viper. He knew whose fault this was: this act of atrocity. Ahead, Mr X chanted on. Screams echoed through the dark, dank cave as his eyes glowed bright white, and he spoke:

"Azathoth, Dagon, Nyarlathotep, Yig, Shub-Niggurath, Yog-Sohoth, Cthulhu."

A dense fog seemed to be entering the room. Alex choked as its ghastly aroma reached him, retching. It smelt like blood.

"You are in my world now, and you shall never leave."

"The puzzling enigma is within your souls, I will bring your greatest fears."

He turned to Anya. *"The girl still running from Dad."* He turned and stared at Shea . . . *"or maybe me"* . . . to Charlie *"So much fire . . ."*

Then, finally, he turned to Alex and, in a cold voice that left frost in mid-air, spoke:

"Murderer."

INTO THE CAVE

S HEA, BARELY CONSCIOUS, and with no voice, began to panic. The tablets on the walls had begun to engrave themselves. Symbols began to form; lines and curves, with no obvious meaning.

Suddenly, as the last word left the man's lips, his form contorted, and he threw himself on the floor. A dense fog was choking the room. She could barely breathe! Everyone else seemed to have passed out. Several lights entered the room, running right into the man then ricocheting off to each tablet. The ground shook in protest, the walls cracking under the pressure. The room veiled itself in darkness. Lights flickered; red lines streaking across from wall to wall while Mr X writhed and screamed. Then a bright light exploded from the centre, and she passed into darkness.

Alex

Before he could say anything, Alex appeared back in his old room. A young boy was sitting on the bed. It looked like him. On the boy's lap was an open book, blank sheets of paper waiting. There was a pen in his hand.

Alex gaped. It *couldn't* be him . . . it was just . . . how had he even got here? He stared at the young boy. Red had flushed his face; he looked angry. Grimacing, the boy put his pen to the white sheets. Alex was to witness himself writing in his journal. He knew what he had wrote. A surge of panic ran through him like electric. Desperately he began shouting, willing himself to stop.

"Don't write that! Stop, you don't know what you're doing!"

Alex turned and ran downstairs, just in time to see the Red Caps. There they were, killing his parents, all over again. Alex looked at the tangled mess of limbs and blood on the floor of his kitchen; people that no longer even looked human. The Red Caps stood above, eyes glinting with glee as they gorged on the pooling liquid, letting it run in rivulets from their cheeks. Alex stared in horror. He felt ill. Shaking with sickness, he raised his fist as he struck the Red Cap on his Dad . . . but his hand just went through, as if he was a ghost.

Alex fell to the floor, crying, whimpering.

"I couldn't stop them," he sobbed, hysterically, "Please! *I couldn't stop them!*"

Anya

Anya, back in Russian, sees herself as an 11 year old again. Above her is her father, standing with her, his hands on her shoulders.

"What was *Viktoriya* doing round *here*?" she heard the man ask, poison in his voice. It was a tone completely different to that he'd used only minutes ago, when he'd held her tight. It was a tone full of anger, of rage. Of vengeance.

"It was an accident." she heard the child say.

Anya watched, heat rising in her back, as the giant pulled the girl from his grasp and stood up. He was tall, intimidating by anyone's standards. Anger boiled on his face, a rage terrible and true.

"I thought we told you not to bring your clumsy friends round here!" he snarled, while she, the child, stood dumbly, powerless and terrified under his sudden terrible glare. "Don't tell me your mum said we could have her!"

The young girl gaped silently, like a fish out of water, struggling for the words that would protect her mother.

"TELL ME!"

Anya feels sick. Her heart is pounding-head rushing. She knows what will happen. Then her father grabs her, gripping her tightly by the hair, raising one clenched fist high above her, and she hears her own screams of pain as the young child begins to struggle. A sick cold feeling washes over her.

Then . . . something happens. Anya found herself moving; moving swiftly, with no control over direction. She is zooming towards her father, to her, sees herself open her eleven year old mouth in a scream . . . and she is inside, looking up at her father with great beastly eyes. But she does not feel eleven. She does not feel scared. All she feels right now, is anger. She will end this now. It's her turn to hurt, her turn to abuse. Hot and shaking, she raises her fist . . . and the whole scene drops out of sight.

Charlie

Charlie walked into the room, slammed the door and slumped across his chair. He felt dazed. The world seemed to swim before him. He put a hand to his sweating forehead, bringing it away to show a shining wet palm. He looked up, out a cross the shining room out of the wide wised windows across New York City. wait. What was that? something was hurtling towards him. Something at the speed of lightning. Charlie squinted across the sunlit room. What the . . . ? What was it? It was . . . . Oh GOD!

In the split second that he remained conscious, Charlie can remember only two things-a horrid, sinking feeling as a colossal jumbo jet soared towards him at over 400 miles per hour, pilot still firmly strapped in, eyes wide with horror, and a sudden burning, aching excruciating pain, more powerful and blinding than anything he had ever felt before. His eyes popped, blood vessels screaming as coloured circles flickered and vanished. A high pitched scream, so loud he thought his skull would shatter. A shriek of glass, a sudden image of a blood-stained man, slumped against a high backed chair . . . and then no more.

Charlie awoke to a sickening burning feeling in his abdomen. His eyes blurred and flashed. His head span, he reeled over to be sick, and placed his hand is something that was astoundingly hot. Snatching his hand away, he realised he was surrounded with flames. Flames as high as the office ceiling, bearing down on him. He opened his dry mouth to scream, and instantly inhaled a mouthful of smoke. Coughing and blinded, he stood. His head reeled and he thought he was going to collapse. Got to get out, he thought, blindly, staring around at the mass of flame licking the walls. He turned. There was a gap to his right. He ran through. Flames missed his foot by inches, scorching heat running across the soles. Charlie could feel it in his toes, but couldn't tell whether he was on fire or not. His whole body felt numb, sickening, out of control. There was a sudden scream and the sound of a crashing window. He reached the door and pulled it open, heart racing, and there was another sound of breaking glass. Suddenly Charlie felt tired, but for some reason his legs pulled him forwards and he had a dim vision of pitching down the stairs. A woman stood at the platform, arms tangled around the banister, head down. Charlie pulled her arm, and she stumbled, falling almost head first. He let go, and ran down the second flight, the third, the forth, aware at each moment that he was leaving good people behind. There was the sound of an explosion, and Charlie pitched headfirst across the floor, rolling onto his back. Legs jumped over him, high heels ran past. Charlie writhed, avoiding the stampede then rolled back onto his stomach. There was a sudden explosion from above. Charlie remembers a dull thud across his back. And then . . . nothing.

Shea

Flames flickered from the candles' wicks, held by men in dark grey robes. They followed a tall, shrouded figure up the marble staircase, and entered a room with seven tablets held against seven walls. Each of the figures placed themselves by a tablet, arms out towards a centred black figure. The chanting began. The man in the centre chanted louder than the others, repeating several words, words that the others weren't saying.

"Azathoth, Dagon, Nyarlathotep, Yig, Shub-Niggurath, Yog-Sohoth, Cthulhu."

Over and over the words sounded. Not words, but names. As each name was repeated, the tablets began to engrave themselves. Symbols began to form; lines and curves, with no obvious meaning.

Suddenly, as the last name left the black man's lips, his form contorted, grew larger and more ghastly. Several lights entered the room, running right into the man then ricocheting off to each tablet. The ground shook in protest, the walls cracking under the pressure. The men screamed and fled, leaving his black spirit to spread himself around the room, veiling it in darkness.

In the middle, Shea's eyes widened as the view grew suddenly darker. She felt like she was choking, suffocating in what could only be described as poison. Her mind was giving out, screaming, screaming louder and louder, waiting for the blackness to stop. She was struggling to breathe. Darkness overcame her, and she blacked out.

THE GREATEST
TERROR

WRAPPED IN A world of confusion, Alex looked up to see an outline of a tall man. A face swam into his image, blurred at the edges. Somewhere distant, a hollow echoing was growing louder and louder, as though he were surfacing from great depth. He became aware of his limbs, and the cold, aching ground he was lying upon. His mind whirred: he could not remember why he was on the floor. He looked up to see a mysterious man, with writing spread across his face. He was getting clearer and clearer; now he was almost whole. The echoing was growing louder still: a great harrowing scream of delight, that rang like alarm bells in his ears. Alex looked around, half expecting to see his parents. But his parents were dead, and that man had been in his dream, and . . .

A memory like a flash of lightning raced in front of him, making him re-live his terrible nightmare. But now Alex recognised him. Anger flooded him. He struggled to his feet. It was clear.

"It was you!" he told the demon; the man he had just seen in his dream; the same man that stood before him now. "You left me that book, and you killed my parents!"

Then, suddenly, it was over, and Alex was back in the room, shaking, and angry as he had ever felt in his life. He stood up, drenched, and ran at Mr X. He did not care what would happen; all he knew was raw pain: anger that seeped through every fibre in his body. He wanted to hurt; to kill. He raised a sturdy fist,, and brought it crashing down on the figure, but to his blind confusion, his hand slipped through. He tried again. It was like touching cold air. Alex could see him, why was he not there? His sturdy grasp was useless against nothing. His great strength could not touch him.

"You can't hurt him." came a voice, but Alex barely heard. He struck again, and still nothing happened. Mr X stood, laughing viciously, loud and cynical, taunting Alex as his futile blows hit nothing.

"Why?!" he screamed. "WHY DID YOU DO IT?! WHY DID YOU WANT THEM?! THEY WERE NOTHING TO YOU! NOTHING! AND YOU . . . YOU . . . I'LL *KILL* YOU!"

"You can't!" came a cry, as Mr X's laugh ran louder, high-pitched and menacing.

"*What do you mean?!*" panted Alex, rage coursing through him. He raised his fist again. He did not care what kind of demon he was. He wanted to hurt . . . to kill him . . .

"He is only like a shadow." echoed the voice. It came from the girl. From where he was stood, Alex could see her, shackled against the wall, trapped behind her captor. It was like he was staring through water. He tried the blows again, fists raised, determined to make him suffer.

"You can't stop him."

Mr X's laughed was bouncing off the walls, ricocheting in a sickening spiral that left his high cold laugh reeling in Alex's mind.

Blindly, Alex stared around. A sudden, weary feeling overcame him. He was aching all over. His legs felt numb. He felt confusion, like a sudden headache. Was there nothing he could do?

The voice laughed manically in his head. As his vision blurred, Alex watched his friends, writhing on the floor. It was like time itself had slowed. Anya's face was contorted in agony, Charlie's mouth was open wide, his lips blood-red in a final silent scream. He didn't understand any more what was going on. He didn't know, in fact, why he was here at all, or who these people were, or what he was doing. Then suddenly Anya screamed; a sickening cold scream that broke the demonic cackling like it had come from the very pit of Hell, and Alex, almost bent double in his weariness, remembered. Somewhere, out of his mind so far that it could have been a very distant voice, there was a sudden clearness. This man was not human. He, Alex was not human. While still in human form, he could not prevent the apocalypse. He could not prevent Hell. He looked back over at Shea. All that time he had spent, hiding from her, hoping she would not recognise his strength and speed as being only part-human. But now was not the time for pride, or pretence. They needed him. He had to do it.

He stood swaying and walked slowly towards his friends. His vision was so blurred he could now only make out their outlines. Behind him, Mr X screamed with joy. But he wasn't walking away.

He stopped. He turned. In his daze, he knew only the sickening sense of pride and honour that overwhelmed him. Well, then, this was it; goodbye world.

He took one last final breathe, and began to run. His feet picked up speed, brushing the cold stone floor. His torso bulged. On his arms and legs, Alex could feel thick fur sprouting, growing uncontrollably, wrapping itself around him. His face felt stretched, painfully, his snout growing, teeth spouting like daggers from aching gums, eyes bulging. Up ahead, Alex saw Mr X's face change. The laughed subsided. Alex's feet pushed him forwards; he was running at full speed now, and no-one could stop him. On all fours he was stronger. He felt powerful. This was it.

With one wild, unearthly howl, he threw himself at the cloaked figure: torturer, and murderer.

Suddenly the cave exploded. A large red pool spread across the floor. Alex was falling, clinging to the ghastly garment that connected him and his enemy. He looked down. Below he could see islands, floating, black and red, tinged, levitating in a blood-red sky.

Then the floor reappeared, and they were no more.

ONE MAN DOWN

S HEA WOKE TO find herself back on the cold stone floor. The room was eerily silent. She lay, shaking, feeling sick. To either side of her, lay Charlie and Anya, their faces pale, their eyes closed. In her head was a rumbling sound, like a plane. Shea looked up, and stared in horror at what she saw.

The roof was collapsing.

Large cracks appeared in the age-old stone, rifts that determined whether the roof remained over their heads. Plaster had started to fall, raining down on her. She heard a gasp, and turning, found both her companions were stirring. Drowsy and confused, their words were slurred. Shea rushed over, hauling them to her feet with all her might. Small pieces of rubble were now collapsing onto them, covering the floor in a fine dust. It wouldn't be long before the larger chunks followed. They needed a way to escape; *anything* would do. Staring wildly around, Shea managed to locate the nearest door; a heavy wood one, underneath the arches. She grabbed Anya's arm, and pulled. She was heavy, and the drowsed look on her face told Shea she was oblivious to the danger surrounding them. Dragging her, and a semi-conscious Charlie, with some unknown strength of the gods, she rushed over and tried to tug it open, pulling desperately at the golden hoop, but it didn't budge. She pulled harder. Two hands lost their grip as Shea put her might to the structure, but it didn't move an inch. The door seemed to be locked. Larger, stone like pieces were now tumbling to earth. Their time was running out. A hand appeared at her side: Charlie seemed to have come to, and was pushing at the door, looking increasingly panicked as he came to terms with the new, frightening situation he found himself in.

"I think it's locked!" Shea shouted, trying to make herself heard over the blast of rubble as rock hit the cold floor, but Charlie did not stop. In a barely concealed bewilderment, he had begun foraging in his pocket.

What was he doing?

More rubble crashed the floor; bigger, and more deadly. Charlie drew a thin piece of bent metal, raised it up the lock, peering in. Now Anya seemed to be coming to life; Shea felt the arm in her hand pull away, and noticed she was now staring about the room with a look of both confusion, and panic.

"You can't move it!" shouted a voice from somewhere. The two of them glanced around, but the shouting continued. A large slab fell to the floor, crumbling with a deafening blow. Someone screamed, a scream that pierced their ears, making them turn in terror. Beyond the falling mass, Charlie could see a figure, writhing and thrashing against the walls, seemingly unable to set itself free. A block descended, hitting the floor and exploding only inches away, showering the figure in a cloak of white dust. Charlie's eyes darted about, trying to see the best way through.

Who was it?

It was obviously a person. It had to be-no other creature he knew of could scream so gut-wrenchingly as that. Next to him, Shea's hands scratched uselessly at the door. Anya too, was attempting the same, tears running down her face as she realised what little chance they had.

"Don't worry!" he tried to shout, but the crashing was too loud. Any second, there was going to be an avalanche.

Charlie took a deep breath, and leapt through. His head was in a daze, like he was back in that office, like it was all happening again, but he kept on leaping, fighting his will to run. On the other side the crashing became deafening as he reached the creature, and from his belt pulled a magnificent grey pick. Up, up in the air it went. He saw the girl's face flinch, eyes closed, fearing the worst. Then he brought it crashing down. There was a searing noise, like a knife through skin. He opened them, and saw the girl dashing through the torrent of plaster, leaping like her life depended on it. Charlie jumped, following her, trying not to think, blocking his thoughts. The door seemed an age away, as if the room had somehow expanded. He ducked and swayed, his ears suddenly filled with white noise, no longer awake to the catastrophe surrounding him. Then, like a slow motion movie, he was there. Charlie put his boot on the wall, gripped the handle, and pushed as hard as he could ever muster. His muscles screamed in rage, but he did not care. They would all die in this hell of a place. Slowly the door opened. There was a crashing sound. Shea pushed Anya through, before her, and just as they reached the other side, a large crunching sounded.

They fled. Passages that seemed to make no sense sent them in oblique directions; they hit a dead end, and a hasty retreat was made, as they scarpered back down the nearest alley, with no clue as to whether they had already been that way or not. All they could hear was the crashing behind them as stone and mortar fell, ready to strike down any innocent victim who came behind one step too late.

Shea could not remember running faster. Her mind seemed to have gone on auto-pilot. Whatever she was doing was not in keeping with her brain. She could not even tell whether she was with the others any more; they seemed to disappear, then come into view again in a haze of grey dust. Ahead of her Charlie came in and out of vision; panicking, running blindly, shouting things she could not hear. They hit another dead end. A left, a right. They were running; running blindly, trying to escape something she knew they couldn't. Above her something cracked. Small rubble showered in her eyes, blinding her, and she leapt, her ears open to a sharp crunching as the roof gave way. Behind her a sudden booming shot around the chamber. Something heavy hit the floor, sending deafening tenors ringing into her ears. Her arms flailed. She wasn't going to make it. Then something hit her back, and she went flying. Fearful and lost, Shea saw the ground speed towards her, saw it face to face. Then she saw nothing, but a bright light, and finally darkness.

Shea woke to find herself in a very bright place. In fact, it was extremely bright, much brighter than the cave had been. Whiteness pressed against her. She blinked, and something soft landed on her nose, making a tingling fuzz. It must be cold. She tried to move her arms, but they seemed hollow, and somewhat disconnected. Then another landed on her cheek, then another.

If this was Heaven, then it was very cold. Not only that, but it was also slightly annoying. Cold fingers brushed her cheek, touching her skin. She wanted to push them away. She reached out at her shoulder, and saw with surprise that the hand that swam in front of her wore gloves. Not only that, but it was small, and somehow connected to a very horrible orange something, that puffed out in great rings in a line beyond it. She tried to wave it in front of her, and the gloved hand obeyed.

Did Heaven know about orange? Did it know about gloves? And if so, why was everything else white? Shea turned her head, and found with willing ease her neck obeyed. Beyond her lay two figures, dancing strangely in the white, their backs twisted in a sudden dance of joy. But something was wrong. The figures were not moving, and now she saw they were frozen, solid, jumping in mid-air. Shea lifted her head, reaching for any signs of life, of mere existence, and a coolness seeped down her neck. The whiteness was not the background she had thought, but globules of snow; sticking to her hair, numbing her ears, freezing her mind. Then she remembered.

It was like a dream. Shea lay there, waiting for the feeling to return to her limbs. It was slow, and painful. She stood up and brushed herself down, steadying herself. Before them, just beyond her head, large grey boulders blocking the entrance. There was no way back.

Around her, the rest of the team got slowly to their feet. Dazed, bruised and battered, but still intact, they stood, and stared at the death-trap that lay before them.

There was a moment of silence. None of them, who stood on that icy precipice, could believe it. The castle had collapsed, almost right on top of them. By pure fluke, or charm, or luck they did not know, but they had somehow managed to get out. Before them, the icy stones stood silent, already embraced by the whipping winds, claiming them for their own.

"Come on." Shea said, finally, breaking the strange atmosphere that had crept into the air. She supposed they *had* to go back. They'd lost the dagger, somehow they were missing a team member, and completely ruined a damned good opportunity. And, to make things worse, if they didn't move soon, the Red Caps would return, and that really would finish them off. Mr X had disappeared, the portal had closed, and Shea had run out of ideas. It was back to the boardroom.

Wearily the crew gathered in silence, defeated. No-one appeared to have any energy. It was like the joy had been somehow sucked out of them, as if they had just been through something terrible but could not remember what. In her mind, Shea, becoming ever-more conscious in the biting winds, knew the only thing they could do now was to return; to rest their weary minds. Anya did not even seem to notice they were one down.

Charlie, staring at the vast emptiness, knew the portal had closed. He had seen it, just before the room had turned to blackness. He knew what Alex had done; seen him change. His best friend was gone, and he was experiencing a sick, empty feeling he'd never felt before. He wondered if Shea knew; stealing a quick glance at her weary face, he supposed not. He thought of looking for Alex, sick thoughts running through his head, though in his mind he knew what had it was hopeless. He'd seen them fall; seen the pure rage that had fled the demon, only to be replaced in his friend. He knew, better than anyone else stood on that icy peninsula, what it meant now Alex was gone.

A LIFE FOR A LIFE

C HARLIE LOOKED ACROSS. There stood the girl-an untouchable image, standing with her arms wrapped around her thin body, her soft hair whistling in the oncoming flurry of snow. He watched as a dirty yellow streak slipped across her cheek, revealing a damaged, broken face, flawed with deep scars and remorse. Through her thin faded top, Charlie could see her ribs. In his head he heard Shea sigh. He watched her approach the girl, speaking in soft tones.

"Hello. My name is Shea. You must be very cold."

The girl stared at her. She did not answer.

"Would you like my coat?"

Again, the girl did not answer, but Charlie thought he saw the faintest jerk of a nod. Shea wrapped the coat around her, then kneeling on the floor set down her pack and fetched out boots.

"Always carry spare. Never know when you might need them."

Charlie tried to smile, but it felt as if his jaw had stuck. There was something terribly tragic about the girl he had just saved. It was as though she was almost a replacement. But Charlie, standing there with his back to the arctic wind, did not think he could ever replace Alex. She was silent, cold as the snow that stung his cheeks, making him forget the rashness and brutality of the last few minutes. It was as though a deep silence had descended upon them, closer than his own skin. He winced and turned away, not willing to watch as Shea gently tugged the girl into more suitable attire.

From the ground, Anya knew that something was very wrong. She did not recall the last few minutes. All she knew is that she and Charlie had been in the cave one minute, and the next they had been zooming like lightning down terrifying dark passageways, listening to the manic bodiless laughter as something choked her.

Confusion. A dark cave, white light. Then . . . Anya gulped. It was like she had fallen into a dream. A long, deep, sickening dream from which she could not wake. She remembered her father had been in it. Then reality hit her like a stone, and she gulped back strong tears. Yes, she remembered it; everything he'd done. Just as he had been about to do it; to penetrate her childish innocence with one sickening brutal act, something had happened. There had been a cold, flawless light. A blinding light. Her body had felt cool and her mind had been free. She had felt . . . elevated, floating along, somehow disconnected from all those around her, free of her troubles, looking down onto the perfect world below. Then someone had called her name, and she had woken to the sound of thunder, Shea's cries ringing as she struggled with an unmoving door, more solid than anything Anya had ever felt. Anya had only just realised in time that she had actually been trying to open it. Then it had been a blur. She remembered grey, and a feeling of almost emptiness. Now she was back on the barren earth. The coldness was snow. The emptiness was the emptiness of her own soul, her whole entire being. She looked up. From her kneeling position, she could see Shea attending someone. She turned around. There was Charlie; she remembered him now, wrapped in his Michelin jacket, hat pulled down across his forehead, eyes barely visible. So where was . . . ? Anya could not see Alex. She remembered, at least, there had *been* someone called Alex. He was a boy, but she could not think what age, or how tall he was, or even how she knew him. Still, there was no-one else; it was only the four of them.

She stood up, and her muscles suddenly ached as she felt something heavy across her back. She reached behind, and her hands caught canvas. It was a rucksack.

Suddenly Anya remembered. Yes, there was someone called Alex. She spun around again, as if expecting him to suddenly appear, but all she could see were miles and miles of snow.

Charlie watched her sadly as she turned, bewildered.

"He's not here!" he cried across the bracing winds, snatching his words.

"Who isn't?" she called back.

"Alex!"

"Why?!"

"He went into the portal with Mr X!"

"With who?!"

"Mr X!"

"Oh right!"

Anya did not remember a Mr X, but she gathered that Alex was at least not here. Ahead, the girl had changed attire completely. Shea marched up to her, her green eyes poking over the top of a balaclava. Anya's mind whirred. She could remember . . . something . . . the riddle, the curse . . . *to take the blood of that which stole, will open up the portal hole . . . .* that was it! And the last person who reportedly took it, had been called . . .

"We've got to go!" Shea shouted in muffled tones, indicating at the clad stranger. "Charlie rescued Grace! That's her name! I get it now! It's in the legend-the legend in that book! He needs her blood! It's an ancient curse-you've got to have a special kind of blood. You took the dagger from him at some point-you must have, so only he can take it, and the blood, from you! Mr X still exists, he'll be after us! We've got to get back across the lake!"

Anya nodded, and tried to catch Charlie's eye as the wind buffeted her. It was coming down in a storm now, whistling its way across the open plain, pushing them onwards. She knew-could also sense it in her-that they were in danger, though she could think why. She saw Charlie turn to the wind, and they set off, trudging their boots across the thick blanket, leaving no trace as the snow covered their footfalls behind.

The walk was treacherous. The merciless wind, buffeted them from every angle, forcing them to wander blindly. Shea's tracker kept on beeping, causing anxiety to spread like a storm cloud across the whole group. Ahead, they kept the girl in their sight; she walked amazingly well for someone whose face made it look like they had not eaten in the past month. Anya could still not really remember who she was. All she knew was they needed to keep walking-needed to find somewhere to shelter, but her body ached and she longed to stop, willing to curl into a ball in the cold, soft snow.

At the bottom of a steep incline, they came to a rest in a small cave, found by Shea's device. Pitifully, the group dumped their bags. Grace took Alex's, settling down in absolute silence, though Charlie doubted she would sleep.

No-one spoke as they unrolled kit, and climbed in fully clothed. Slowly, secluded, cut-off from one another, each nodded into a different, separate world, and they slept, fretfully, dreaming to keep out the cold that shook them in their sleeping bags.

Eventually, morning broke. Awake, Charlie sat, listening to the howling wind. Across the cave in the semi darkness, he lit a torch and found Grace, lying still, her eyes open wide. He tried to catch her eye, but they seemed glazed, and she did not seem to recognise him. He wondered if he should make breakfast. The others were still there, sleeping peacefully on the floor, as the snow still whipped around the cave entrance, sending shivers up his spine. Since he was not alone, and this girl, Grace, had evidently been starved, he supposed he'd better try.

Rummaging in his backpack, all he could find were a tube of dextrose tablets. He took one, and threw the rest across to her, but she did not react. They tasted sweet, artificially so. He rubbed the grains along his tongue and swallowed. All he could do now was wait. He looked back across at the girl. She seemed to have noticed the package, though she did not seem to to want to look at it. Her glazed eyes flickered and stared across the barren floor. Oh well, at least she was alive. Charlie shrugged, and turned his back, partly so she could eat if she wanted, and watched the storm outside. Snow swathed in the entrance and light fragments danced in the winds. By the time Shea and Anya woke, it had grown calmer, and whiteness had settled once again. They took poor remnants for breakfast and set off into the bright light, heading for the mountains.

Scaling them this side was not any easier. It was hard. Cold. Ice chipped into them, and Anya's backpack pulled her down. The other two were helping Grace. They had no choice but to climb. Whiteness pressed on her brain, sharp stabs of pain as her body struck rock. They ought to have used ropes, but they were mainly in Alex's pack, and they were without him now.

Finally, the ledge was reached. The exhausted team hauled themselves over, panting. Together they looked out across the other side, staring down at the vast green sea that was the lake.

CTHULUS AGAIN

A T THE TOP of the mountain, they collapsed, and lay on the cold ice surface, feeling their breath leaving their bodies in icy bursts, their chests rising and falling. Charlie's side ached, as if he had stitch. Snowflakes began to fall again, touching his nose and brushing his cheek. It was a sweet coldness, promising of peace. They lay for quite some time, swimming almost into unconsciousness, before jerking themselves back to the soothing plateau, resisting the temptation to fall into a final sleep in the swirling whiteness. They had made it. Top of the mountain. Below, Charlie could hear a rippling breeze, and remembered with a dull vagueness of the lake they had still yet to cross. He felt so peaceful. Whiteness pressed against his eyes when he closed them, and he felt himself slipping into a balmy slumber. It was like he was floating. Below, a pulling breeze was rippling the waters. They still had yet to cross it. Charlie's mind drifted. He felt content, like he was suddenly in a very happy place. He didn't know where it was, but it was the most comfortable, warm, soothing place he'd ever been in. His mind went blank as his thoughts faded away. None of them were important any more.

Someone shook him rudely, and Charlie's eyes sprung open. It was like being jumped in a hospital. He felt like he'd received a huge electric shock that had coursed right through his body. The soothing feeling fled as he watched Anya peer over him, her dark hair and pale face tucked behind a hat, hood, and black scarf that dangled, brushing his chest.

"Are you okay?"

A feeling of annoyance rose in Charlie's chest. Of course he was okay! He'd just been in the happiest place in his life! He quickly closed his eyes, trying to recapture the feeling, but it had gone. He felt Anya's hand on his shoulder, presumably about to shake him again, and sat up, eyes closed, staring blindly ahead. Anya watched in confusion as he stumbled to his feet, and blinkingly opened his eyes to the flurrying snow. A short while away, a small clad figure was pulling at Shea's coat. She turned, and Grace appeared to whisper something to her. There was a short silence, hindered only by the soft whistle of the rushing snowflakes. Charlie could see her thinking, her face contorting as she tried to figure something out.

"I . . . yeah, it would work. Can you do it?"

Grace nodded.

"Right. Listen, Grace has an idea. It's brilliant. She thinks it's got the magic."

Shea reached into her coat with a black-gloved hand, and pulled out the amulet that Charlie had stared at so long ago. Pulled from her neck, it always burned bright, even in the glowing dullness of the day. Its bright diamond scarred his eyes, gleaming in the swirling whiteness.

"I didn't realise it at the time, but it does have magical properties. Apparently, we don't have to just blind them this time. I thought the shock was just-well, whatever. We think, well I think, with the magic of being round Mr X for so long, I think Grace can control things: just like Mr X did with the

Red-Caps. I think it rubs off. I'm not sure how long for, but if we can get one of them down there, we can hitch a ride back across, yeah?"

Charlie wasn't so sure. Much though he hated to think it, she sounded desperate more than anything. Staring down into the vast abyss, he could make out the soaring shapes. They looked small; but he knew that was an illusion. It wasn't even something he'd thought of; he'd been so preoccupied climbing the mountainside, he had given even the slightest though to what might be over the ledge.

They'd have to descend, but how to do so without being seen?

An eerie screech spread over the lake, warning the trespassers away. Below, the monsters stood, beating their great leathery wings in the non-existent sun, twenty feet high; again the large dragon-like creatures of nightmares, bodies of green and a tail, a green, ghastly tail with points as sharp as knives.

Stood at the top, they drew back as Grace stood alone on the precipice, holding the talisman forth, its bright jewel catching the snowy drift and glimmering eerily in the whiteness. Below another screech followed, and the crew shivered in the silence that seemed to have enmeshed them in its trap. The talisman glimmered, casting a sudden glare over the barren landscape. Shea strained her ears; there was the cold brush of wind, and her own quiet breathing.

No: there was something more. She could hear . . . it sounded like, almost like, a helicopter, getting closer; the consistent purring of the spinning blades. It was getting louder, and Shea listened closely to the soft beating pattern. She looked about, but the sky was white as dew, and she realised with a jolt the only thing it could possibly be was the sound of beating wings.

Something erupted over the precipice, only feet from where Grace stood, isolated and vulnerable on the cliff face. It let out a harrowing noise, that echoed in the distant valley and made Shea's blood run ice cold. It was like the sound of death; of the eagle, hunting it's unfortunate prey; a sound that made fear run in thin lines of panic through her stomach and spine, paralysing her in terror. The creature dived, suddenly, seemingly out of nowhere, wings beating. Down it plundered, rising to her beating heart, her breath rising in an icy mist. She could not move. All she could see was its cold, bare teeth, and snarling nostrils, below its fiery amber eyes.

A glimmer caught her trapped vision. The monster screeched and rose upwards, twisting, spiralling, screaming as the brightness burned and seared. It dived again, contorting like a puppet, lustful for revenge.

"DUCK!" someone screamed and Shea found herself flat on the soft floor, inhaling the thick white powder. Above, the monster turned, thrashing wildly, fighting control. Brightness seared across its brain, causing a sharp whiteness, blurring its crystal vision. Below, the small figure stood defiant, holding out the dazzling ray. Then its pupils shrunk, and it began to fall, limbs flailing as it lost control, belly upwards, wings no longer of use. The small figure flung the jewel sideward, as the creature thrashed, motioning it to a swift descent, flipping it over, leading its path to glide softly onto the cool landing strip.

Now they could get across. Anya rose from her cold position and stared uncertainly into its now enlarged pupils. The creature let out a squawk and shuffled forward. She could not believe it was now tame; she remembered the panicked thrill she had first felt when she had first come across them in her book; they were rarely seen; and anyone who did see them were unlikely to survive the sighting. Another, recovered by police from a raid on a murderous cult, had "represented a monster of vague outline, but with a scaly, rubbery-looking body, prodigious claws on hind and forefeet, and long, narrow wings." They had once been quoted by a stunned trekker as 'a human caricature . . . . A pulpy, tentacled head surmounted a grotesque scaly body with rudimentary wings.'

Yes, they were lethal. No doubt about it. And now they had to get on its back.

They scaled up the magnificent beast; trying to grasp its soft skin. Warmth radiated from the creatures hide; once again, Charlie was surprised to find its vulnerable need for heat, rather than a frigid exterior as cold as its heart; to find it was, somewhere inside, still yet in possession of the substance known as living. He arched himself along the great creature's spine, soon sandwiched between Grace and Anya as they clambered up. Then, with its vast beating wings wide, the creature raised its head, and they hovered inches from the ground. Charlie felt insecure, like a child on a see-saw with an older, much heavier kid, afraid of the sudden jerk that would send him sailing to the icy waters thousands of feet below. He screwed his eyes shut tight, trying to stop the whistling wind that seemed to be turning them to icy marbles.

Suddenly they were out across the ocean, blank waves pulsing below in a never-ending ebb. They ducked and swerved along a relentless jet stream, hurtling towards the icy waves, pulling up in a gravity-defying wrench. The beating wind screamed in their ears almost to the point of madness. They clung on desperately, clasped to hope, the green scales seamless against their skin, plunging headfirst towards the snow, and in blind panic all four shut their eyes. The streaming wind bore no grace against them, rushing past them in an icy torrent, like angels snatching them with frail fingers up to a land above.

Then, with a rise, and a thud, they reached touchdown. Charlie swung sideways, and fell onto land. His back hit the coldness. Above him, the air fuzzed with electricity, and he closed his eyes, not seeing Grace as she warded the creature away. When he opened them again, it was gone. A hollow nothingness was left in the air where it had stood and he had lay next to foot-long talons. A breathtaking peacefulness had once again stolen over his mind, and he lay, succumbing to its power, glad for the first time in days that he was alive.

THE LAST LEG

S HEA WOKE AT an unknown time. She stared blankly at the dark green canvas, that held her tight again the snow. In the middle of it all, they'd managed to end the day in a forest-something that had been completely unknown to them on their trek north. They wouldn't have found it had Anya not insisted Shea looked on her laptop for shelter. It was obvious she had been worried about Grace-she kept casting odd, sideways glances, as if wondering if she'd fall. The girl was painfully thin, and no-one had let her carry anything. The forest was a god-send, but to get back out again they'd have to endure yet more walking. Great. She rolled over. Anya was still asleep, her brown hair cascading across the hood of the sleeping bag, covering most of her face. After about half an hour of lying there, she began to stir. Shea prayed momentarily that she wouldn't wake, delaying the dreaded task ahead, but Anya opened her eyes and smiled blearily at her, before rolling over and making no sound at all.

Shea knew they should be gone in the next half hour, and rolling over, freed herself of her twisted sleeping bag. She dressed, and feeling a little better, unzipped the tent as quietly as she could, Anya groaned as cold air swept over her, huddling closer to the thin walls. Shea stepped out and re-zipped the tent, blinking in the fresh light. No movement from the orange tent. She looked down-several bottles stood upright, half-filled with water. Some lay scattered on the ground, rolling in a semi-circle. Shea picked them up. It would be no good if someone else came out and knocked them over. There wasn't really a lot of water, but it was a lot better than nothing. In the middle of doing just this, she heard the sound of a tent unzipping. She looked up, to see Grace, huddled in an oversized fishing mac, and smiled. Her stomach rumbled. Hunger, again. They'd have to collect or starve.

"Just going to get some food." she motioned.

Grace nodded. Since she had suggested using the diamond, she seemed to have grown a voice. Shea thought it still must be very confusing, being rescued by a group of total strangers. Still she seemed to be bearing up well.

"I'll come with you. Charlie's not awake yet."

Shea smiled. It would be good to have a one-to-one. After all, from what Grace had been through it was hardly surprising how little she had talked yesterday, and Shea wanted to put her at ease.

"I'll just tell Anya." She poked her head inside the tent. "We're going to get food." She told a sleepy Anya. Anya nodded, to show she had heard. Shea re-zipped the tent and grinned at Grace.

"Come on." she said.

They walked together. It was only a little while until they came to the bottom of the pines-their first immediate source of food. Shea didn't exactly know what she was looking for—an animal, perhaps, like a bird, or anything left on the ground. It wasn't really ideal, but you were never going to feed people on less than seventy-five grams of pasta. She looked up. Cones. Not enough. Spiney pines. Hmmm, not really.

"Look!" Grace pointed. Shea sidled round the tree, staring up into the branches. Green needles obscured her vision and threatened to blind her if they fell. Oh yeah! A nest!

"Brilliant!" Shea hugged Grace "Alright. Now we just need to get up there." She turned and sized up the tree. Situation: high and dangerous. They had rope. She'd have to go back and get it, though. She turned to Grace.

"Wait here a min." she said, and scarpered, walking back and unzipping the tent, fumbling in her pack for the long twisted trail of hemp. Anya was still, asleep. Oh, well. Shea rushed back, handing the rope to Grace, who stared at her blankly.

"Tie a knot in it," Shea instructed, excited. "like a noose. Now swing it around, and see if you can get it one that branch." She pointed.

Grace looked up into the thickening foliage, gave Shea another blank look, and began whirling it above her head, like in the nursery rhyme '*helicopter, helicopter, please come down.*' Shea nearly started singing it. Grace whirled the rope and suddenly let go. The end shot up into the pines, and they were suddenly showered with spikes. But the rope was over. Shea fed the other end of the rope through the noose, forming a tight knot that fastened under the branch as she pulled, and Shea began to scramble up like a monkey. Branches buffeted her face and obscured her light. Pines scratched at her hand, as she pulled herself upwards through the fine twists of rope. She blinked furiously in the light, trying not to be blinded as she passed through the many layers. She had to be near. Near. Nearly . . . yes! There it was! A glimpse between two interconnecting branches—a brown mass of twigs sticking out this way and that. She heaved, and her whole body moved skywards, brushing on a spiky branch that showered her arms with needles. There! She peered over the lip of the nest. If there was a bird in it, she didn't want to frighten it silly. She could only imagine her surprise as a great bird shot upwards, ruffled by her sudden appearance and her palms became hot and sticky on the thin rope. *Remain calm*, thought Shea, trying to recollect herself. She peered again. No birds. Instead, three beautiful baby-blue eggs lay nestled in their mothers pouch at the centre of the collection of mud and bark. Shea looked skywards and breathed out a long heavy sigh. *Thank you God*, she mouthed.

Down below Grace had all but lost sight of her friend. She supposed Shea must by now be at least fifty feet high, if not more, suspended by the steady rope that was held safely in her palms. She glanced into the branches, trying to see through them, not daring to move too far, in case she should cause the rope to swing, and dislodge the girl from the tree.

"Got it?" she called upwards.

"Yeah," came a voice-Shea's voice. "Just err . . . hang on . . ."

Shea was quickly coming to realise that she couldn't get down with three eggs and actually hadn't found a way to carry them down without letting go of the rope.

"I'm gonna have to drop them." she called "Can you catch?"

Grace shouted up. She was starving, and she didn't have the strength. At least she was talking now.

"No. I don't want to let go of the rope."

Shea grimaced. She actually hadn't thought about that.

"Right." she called "tell you what, when I tug on the rope, lower me down."

Shea reached out with her left hand and it closed around one of the tiny blue eggs. Right. She didn't have any pockets to put the other two in, either. She pulled. Gently Grace lowered her to the ground, past all the branches she had met coming up, the brittle egg cradled in her arms. Carefully she let it fall, placing it on the hardened earth, and began to haul herself up again. Up, up, up the rope. To the second, and the third.

Three eggs. A meal for three. The fact that there were four of them would have to wait. Three was the best they could do right now.

Shea realised she didn't actually know what time they had left the others or how long they'd been away, so she and Grace walked back, treasure safely stowed in their hands, with the rope over Shea's shoulder in a coil. There. As they neared the camp, they could see that both Charlie and Anya were now awake and up. Charlie was taking down poles, and Anya seemed to be anxiously rooting through bags, probably looking for something to eat.

"Treasure." called Shea as they showed them the eggs.

Quarter of an hour later and the eggs were lying open on the hot burner. They split them equally-each person mouthing down only six or seven bites each. Still, hot egg was so much better than nothing, that none of them felt they had the right to complain. Charlie had poured all the water into one bottle, and a half, and they took down the tents, packed them away, and set off again.

NIGHTWATCH

THEY HAD STOPPED. Charlie had refused to go further.

Shea knew, from looking at him, that she didn't have much of a choice. He looked exhausted, and they had walked for miles without speech. Anya seemed to be doing considerably well, however, and Shea was surprised to see how long she'd held out. She too wore a backpack, almost the same size as herself; the rations and clothing they had left. They were running low on glycogen too-having given two packets to Grace just to get her off the mountains and out of that cave, and Charlie, who swallowed them like sweets. Anya had refused both of hers, giving in when Shea had reasonably pointed out that if she fainted it might take them even longer to get off the mountains-in fact, too long. Hypothermia, frostbite and starvation, were three things that no single member of the team had a desire to experience, and as they *were* a team, it might be best to eat some in their interest. Shea too had swallowed one in preparation of the long hike, but her knees still ached and her head span. The next water stop would be, thankfully within the next two miles, though they could eat snow at any time they liked. She sighed and leaned over her knees, trying to relieve the dead weight on her back. Her legs felt numb-she literally couldn't feel them. Her head too felt numb with walking for so long, and dizzy, and her aching joints warned her that without rest she was going to topple over. Raising her head slightly to look across at the group, light rain splashed in her eyes and slid down her fringe. They were out of the snow zone now. Though still ankle deep, it was getting lighter as they travelled south. Moods had improved now they were heading homewards, motivated by the prospect of warmth, of noise, of living once again amongst people. Shea couldn't help thinking of the shop and what was going on now—if Mr Finchley, boned and wisened as he was, was wondering where she'd got to. Perhaps he thought she'd abandoned him. Well, she'd have to put that right for a start.

The rain going to get heavier. Anya had put her bag down, but was standing upright, a miracle, considering, swinging her arms above her head, stretching, obviously trying to relieve some of the tension in her back.

Shea stared back at the ground. It was still white, but orange and grey stones lay amongst the whiteness, trapped here and there in the mud. She could see where they had walked, their light tracks trailing across white earth, snow boot treads on the surface. She wondered why it didn't snow here anymore. Perhaps it was to do with Mr X.

She straightened up and unclipped her pack. It dropped with a heavy thud, and toppled to its side. Pain eased slowly through her muscles, and she stretched, raising her arms to the greying sky. They were going to have to camp. Either that, or freeze to death. Shea reached down and undid the many clips on her bag, scrabbling for the tent, which she bought out as it flapped and unrolled in the breeze.

Charlie straightened up and pulled at the other side with gloved fingers. It was a slow group effort as they pegged and pulled. One tent. Two. Ready. The only question now was who would sleep where-originally it had been simple-a boy and girl tent. Not now. Shea supposed it didn't really matter-food and water were the next priority. And what did they have left? A packet of pancakes, some pasta, no meat . . . no, none. Knives and forks. A random spoon . . . and that was it.

"What has everyone else got?" she asked.

"A bottle half filled with water." Charlie replied, holding it up.

"Three pancakes and about a hundred grams of pasta." said Anya.

Shea sighed. Well, pasta and pancakes it was. They'd have to save the water and re-use it at the end-snow took too long to defrost, and they had no means of warming it without wasting fuel. It wasn't tasty, but it was their only viable option.

Half an hour later the water was bubbling. In slid the pasta with a gentle 'shhhhh'. Everyone waited, sat hungrily in the awning over the entrance to the tents, keen for a good, proper meal. Together, Charlie and Anya had left their empty bottles out in the rain, stones at the bottom to stop them from falling, in the blind hope they might at least collect a little precipitation. Shea bit her lip-hunger always bought on bad moods and she was determined not to snap. Grace's stomach rumbled loudly, and she turned away.

While the food was still cooking, everyone was quiet, the soft pitter-patter of the rain their only companion, and Anya cast around desperately for something to say to ease the wait. Soon, though, their meal was ready, although to the four hungry travellers, not soon enough, and silence pervaded their meal, as each dug in hungrily, not minding the bland stickiness on their taste buds.

Soon, the light began to fade and there was nothing else to do but go to sleep. Though not much later than five 'o' clock, each found themselves tucked safely into sleeping bags, in rooms lit only by a single torch, which both tents managed to hang above their heads. No-one was yet asleep, except Grace, who curled up like a cat, and was gone within the first five minutes. In the growing darkness that surrounded the camp, Charlie lay, listening to her breathing. All around was pitch, and at last, he decided he may as well save one of their last resources. Silently, he reached to flick off the torch, and quiet lay in the stillness as the minutes ticked by, falling, steadily, to a deep slumber.

ALEX'S HOUSE

THE WEEK DWINDLED into a blurred haze of snow, ice, and cold. Charlie had lost all sense of time. The nearby forest that had sheltered them; that had given them nutrition and rest had long since gone. He didn't know when he was awake or asleep. His boots were permanently fixed to his feet, and he'd been wearing the same clothes for countless, days, so long that they might have been part of his skin.

At least one good thing had come of it. In the midst of having practically nothing to eat, Grace had, somehow, miraculously, managed to put on weight. Charlie didn't know how; he was sure he was at least half the size he was when they had set off, so long ago. Hey were heading for Alex's house-it was the furthest north, and it gave something for them to aim at. Thank god, Charlie thought, he knew his friend didn't lock the door. Still, aiming for his old residence did not help the pain of losing him: it was like being ill, a knowing, burning sensation in his stomach that would not go away. And now they were heading to his place. For such a lifeless existence that Charlie had branded it before, the prospect of that shoddy little cabin was now the only thing keeping him going. And yet . . . to him, losing Alex was like losing a leg, or an arm, or any other sacred part, that he could not possibly function without. And what was he to do when they got back: what then? Would he just have to continue on his own? He could find a new boy, but Alex had been so much more than just an accomplice. It was strange, but now he thought on it, they had almost become . . . friends. And after his house, he just didn't know where. It wasn't up to him anymore. And they still had miles to cover.

It had taken two weeks to get back over the mountains, and another two days to get back through the forest. Now they'd reached it. It had been heaven to see the broken little hut in the middle of nowhere; like a beacon of light. They'd let themselves in, and almost immediately fell asleep, waking to the open sound of birdsong, the grey stone walls and empty fireplace. Slowly they'd become accustomed to it's hospitality. Only thing now was where to go next.

"So, what do we do now?" asked Charlie.

They were sat around the kitchen table. Actually it was the only table available. Upon reaching Alex's cottage deep in the woods the crew had discovered once again a distinct lack of furniture. As it turned out, Alex's alter-ego showed in the décor; there wasn't really much. A single room, holding a table, four chairs, a TV, and only one armchair. 'Living alone for too long', as Charlie put it.

Apart from that, there wasn't really much; the floor had been covered only by a single pink rug, tassels ragged and faded in the light, sitting quietly below a single, solitary bed. Not exactly a hotel by any means. Luckily, it seemed Alex did at least enjoy the odd bits of human life; there was food in the cupboards, even if it was partly out-of-date, and a bathroom with necessities provided.

The others were also sat round the table. Since they had found their refuge, none of them had really come up with any kind of plan. Shea, as usual, was pacing around. Charlie noticed she did this a lot now when thinking-perhaps it was habit, but he thought he should try it some time. Maybe it really did help. He certainly hoped so.

Grace, of course, was unusually sober, and had been since her unceremonious rescue.

Trapped in a room for what they had discovered to be over three years would probably do that to you, particularly if in your spare time you were employed to do a demon's bidding. Let's face it, thought Charlie, what were the benefits? No perks, no holidays, not even anyone to argue with over lunchtime. Hell, it was worse than the job he'd had.

"We've got to find a way to bring him back," Shea was saying. "I mean, if this *is* an alternate world, and all, surely it must be *somewhere* . . . like, somewhere else, and we can find him. There must be other portals. Right?"

Anya nodded. "Yeah, there are. But the problem is where to find them. I've got a map at my house, actually, it's a miracle I didn't think to bring it. All I've got is this: the portal tracker. It detects energy, like radons, and things. I suppose I could track another, but they don't usually occur within fifty miles of each other. Then the problem is getting to them. Some only occur at a set time, like every fifty years or so. Others only occur once. Some never really happen. They start to give out energy but they never form. Some last months, some last years. Some only last for seconds. It's really hard to keep track."

"So how do we know where the present ones are?" asked Charlie.

"We have a database. Keeps track of them all. Detects energy, maps them, and evacuates people at risk. Of course, we don't tell them why. We cover it up with a fake murder or a burst-"

"A fake murder?! What? You murder people fo-"

"No, silly. We just say there's been one. There hasn't really. Or there's a burst pipe. Or a flood. Whatever's suitable."

The group lapsed into silence. Charlie looked across at Grace. She was sitting with her head down, looking at the table. He had a bad feeling she thought it was all her fault. It wasn't of course, and she had never really voiced this opinion, but her general silence and lack of opinion told his intuition that something was bothering her.

"Y'alright?" he asked, reaching a hand across the table.

Grace looked up with startling blue eyes. Charlie noticed she was very pretty, now she'd been scrubbed up and had some decent clothes on her. There was just a general lack of voice. She nodded, and continued to stare at the unpolished wood, lost in a world of her own.

Charlie sighed. Great. So what did they had left? Three members, most of their equipment, a girl who they didn't know and who could barely talk, a lost amulet, quite a hike, and very few ideas. Oh, and an unknown but surely finite amount of time. He tried to push away from his mind the thought that Alex was lost somewhere, possibly tortured, possibly dead, while his three friends were sitting round his mahogany table without a clue. They hadn't even made it home yet. Of course, none of these thoughts made them seem heroic, or intelligent. None of them had voiced that Alex might be dead, though judging by the way everyone was behaving, it seemed like the mourning had already begun.

Charlie pushed his head into his hands and tried to think. So they'd lost the dagger to open portals. Well, what else opened portals?

"Anya, what else opens portals?" he asked.

Anya scowled. She'd already answered this question and she didn't like repeating it.

"I don't know, I told you. There may be other daggers, but I don't know where they are."

Charlie knew why she didn't like answering the question. The fact that they didn't have the dagger meant they couldn't open any portals anyway, even if they found them. Also, the fact that Mr X did, meant he could get out. Not a great combination, Charlie was sure. Particularly if he wanted to use it to take over the world.

Grace shivered slightly, revealing a long line of scars extending in a parallel fashion up her arm. Charlie felt sick. How on earth could anyone do that to another human being? But Mr X wasn't human. He was a maniac, and dangerous. Not to mention conspiring the eventual takeover of human life. It didn't look good.

Eventually, since three days had passed and no-one had come up with any plans, they had all reluctantly agreed to carry on with their journey. The path, they knew was long, but they had done the hardest part. Still, they were all glad to find themselves safely back on firm ground.

The next day they set off. Anya was quite sure it had been easier when they'd driven there. Who knew how long it would take to get to Fort Augustus by foot? Grace, although still weak from her treatment, looked stronger and more robust than she had when they first found her. Still, no-one allowed her to pack anything. Shea studied the map with infinite care and they left the cottage, their safe staging post, prepared and ready to walk for miles and miles.

The first fifteen minutes wasn't bad. No-one said much, but surely there could have been little improvement to the situation. Then, as time passed, the silence became more eerie, the woods more drab. Great trees hulked around them, closing in, making them feel small and trapped. Anya felt almost like crying. Now she truly understood Alex she couldn't stop thinking about him. He hadn't been a bad person. All the haughtiness that time ago in the bar had been for one reason: protection. To protect himself and his race. Mainly it was to stop her tracking him. No wonder he'd been none too happy when she'd threatened to reveal what he was. Still, it had happened in the end, hadn't it? She looked across at Shea, who appeared to be studying the map. Had she known? Then she remembered the shock that had registered on her face when Charlie told her what had happened. No, she didn't know. Of course she'd been told-told ages and ages ago in the bar when they'd had that stupid argument, but she'd never really believed it. All that time he'd been helping her up the mountains, she never really had done. Perhaps she just thought he was strong, or foreign. Anya, with a jolt, suddenly realised after all this time there were so many things she didn't know about her team. And Alex hadn't wanted to give himself away-not until that very last moment; that ultimate proof. So much for friends.

And how was Charlie? So far, she'd been taking care of Grace. She hadn't even looked closely at him-seen that he was alright. Here brain had just been stuffed with thoughts of getting home-of getting somewhere safe for once, of keeping them together and not dying because of Cthulus, or frostbite, or just giving up.

The road ahead was long, winding, and insecure. Tree after tree blocked their path, and they dodged around them so many times it was a wonder they were heading in any direction at all. Finally, after an hour's laborious trekking, in which hardly anyone spoke, they finally came to a fork. A look in both directions told her whichever route they took, it would be long, with unbroken fields and trees on either side. It looked like no-one lived round here for miles. Great.

The team began to walk.

THE RETURN TRIP

"WHERE ARE WE goin'?" Charlie asked Shea, for the umpteenth time.

"My place, Charlie." came the answer from up ahead, two people down the line, "I've already told you that."

"And where's that?"

"Fort Augustus."

"Where?"

"Fort Augustus. Where we left off from."

"Didn't know you lived there too."

Anya turned on him. She was tired, and Charlie was not helping with the pace.

"It's a little way from here."

There was a pause.

"How far?" Charlie asked, one boot ploughing in front of the other. He hitched up the dead weight on his back. It was the question he'd been dying to be answered. If he could, he'd be asking it every ten seconds, like a little child, tired and ready to go home.

"Far enough."

Charlie glared at her back.

"Shea, I'm tired. We've followed this dirt track for how long now?"

Lagging behind, the last one in the group, he stopped, leaning the pack over his knees so as to give his chest a break. Gravel crunched under the tread on his snow boots. It had started to drizzle; light rain soaking slowly through to his already damp and torn t-shirt. Soaked with sweat, he had already pulled his mac off over his head, despite warning looks and a tongue lashing from Anya about the winds they had yet to encounter. Grace stopped too; sodden in the light haze, trudging along in oversized boots across the muddy coloured gravel, leaving trench marks as she went-a reminder of their journey so far. Velvet pines stood tall on either side, dressed in snow and sheltering them mercifully from the worst of the weather.

Shea turned. Charlie had stopped. Her shoulders ached: she too longed to rest but there were many miles yet to cover and they couldn't allow for the bad weather to close in around them. She looked at the sky. All around them black clouds were closing in. They could get a little further-even if it was only half a mile She knew weather like this-Scotland was famous for its drizzle, but when the rains did follow, they came thick and fast. She consulted her watch-it was two in the afternoon. They'd been walking two hours since lunch. What a day. And it wasn't even over. She groaned, trying to think, but her head felt heavy from exhaustion and no conversation.

They'd taken quite a D-tour from the road-side, through a windy path that instead promised shelter through the trees. Unfortunately it had taken them quite off-route too. All of them had walked along in silence, trying to keep their minds off Alex. Shea knew how much of everything they had-how little energy, and food. Charlie would have given up miles ago had it not been for the three girls egging him on. But there was only a little way left now.

"Come on now," she cajoled him gently.

Charlie didn't move. He stood with his head down, breathing. The pack seemed to be big enough to make another of him, but Shea was not deceived. Apart from their tents and tools, they had very little left.

"We got up the mountains."

Charlie shook his head. "We had Alex then." he replied, breaking the silent rule. "Now we don't."

His head dropped again. Suddenly he stood up, pulling on the arms of his pack, unclipping them, and the whole thing dropped to the ground. Grace jumped at the thud, her blue eyes widening in her pale face.

Shea groaned. She didn't want them to stop now; they could get one, maybe two more miles if they really tried before it rained. Or they really would have to set up camp. That might mean yet another day of walking, and she didn't know if she had the physical or mental strength to do that. Still they had a way to go. It was either that, or perish out here. And that didn't look good.

"Come on!" she cried, trying to budge the group. It was more than five miles, but she wasn't going to tell them that. They had to get going, otherwise they'd be stuck here in the storm, and Shea was not ready to do that. God help anyone stuck in the open highlands on a day like today. She dreaded to think how many times Mr Finch had called her, wondering why the phone was off, and why, after almost two solid months, she was not back. The trip had really changed her. She was used to being a tough cookie, but this journey, this whole *event* had really taken it out of her. But there was a time to shine, and hers was now. She had to push them on. Through everything, it had been Alex, or Anya taking the lead. Now they had a different team-member, who had endured not only endless torture, but a damn cold, thirty-plus mile hike back to civilisation. She could not let them give up now.

"We are going this way!" she said, pointedly, and marched on, the others dragging themselves behind, heading for their next point of safety.

SHEA'S PLACE

THE WALK WAS much better this time. Charlie seemed to have somehow managed to give in to her authority. It had taken a short while complaining, and about an hour in hastily erected tents, sheltering from the barrelling storm, but it had been over sooner than she'd thought, and in the window of opportunity that had presented itself, she was pushing them on. Shea knew they only had about five more miles to go until they reached the town. Everyone seemed to be in higher spirits too, after the storm, for although there still wasn't much conversation, it was a lot better than complaining. Every so often they stopped to rest, aware of Grace's gaining, but still painfully stick-thin figure.

Soon they reached the meadows. Wet snow-covered boots steamed in the sun as they trampled through unkept grass. In the distance, a beautiful, quiet little town stretched before them, it's inhabitants unaware of their presence, rooftops basking in the morning sun. Houses lay peacefully, chimneys gently puffing, undisturbed and unriddled by their arrival. On the high-street, matchstick sized shoppers bustled. It was as though nothing had changed.

"Whoa!" called Charlie, as he looked down upon the tidy row of houses, with a school and church, rising high into the air. "I've never seen it from this angle-it wasn't like this when we left."

"Yeah, well," Shea told him, mustering only a very tired smile, "Always looks better coming home. For those who don't know it, Grace, this is where I live. Welcome to Fort Augustus."

They climbed down, and the four bedraggled travellers meandered through an empty road. It was the middle of the day, but everything was rather quiet. No-one that looked their way out of netted windows would have guessed what the travellers had just been through.

"Here we are." called Shea, stopping in front of a little white cottage, nestled comfortably in the middle of a row right in the middle of the town. "My house."

Charlie, not paying attention, would have walked right past it had she not stopped him right there. It was small-petite, overlooked. Rather like his own house, he thought. He hadn't realised until now how much he missed it.

Shea opened the gate and walked down the slate path, kneeling in front of the step. Everyone waited. She stood up, a tiny glint of metal in her hand.

"Never go without an extra key." she remarked, and opened the door.

The travellers fell inside. No-one had ever felt more relieved to be home-even if it wasn't theirs. They pulled off shoes and socks, dropped bags, and fell to an instantly warming, hearty meal of toast, beans, sausages, hoops, and cornflakes, because that's what the cupboards held. Then, they simply lay, exhausted, with no more energy, and fell quickly to unconsciousness on the living room floor-the first true construction they'd slept in for over a month.

No-one could have been more tired.

THE ARGUMENT

"WE ARE NOT using Black Magic!"

It had been almost a week since they'd been back: tired and weary, they had done nothing but sleep. Most of the bags had been emptied now: if only for something to keep them occupied. Everyone still felt tired. Still, that didn't stop them from arguing.

"Why not?" cried Shea, "It's the only way!"

There was a moment's silence. The four warriors were sat at Shea's kitchen table, Friday's light streaming in through its dainty netted window. Grace had a silent, watchful look on her face. Charlie looked puzzled as though he were trying to figure it all out. Shea was tearful; Anya looked angry.

"I'm sorry." she told them, standing at the corner of one of the chairs. "But I refuse-refuse, you hear-point blank to use that stuff. It's lethal."

"But why not?" asked Shea, sudden tears in her eyes, her tiredness still catching up with her emotions. "It's the only way!"

Anya shook her head.

"It's dangerous, it's corrupt, and it's cursed. Even you've told me that! Luck only lends-it doesn't give; ever heard the phrase? Black magic is exactly the same. You think you only skim the surface. Next thing you know you have all sorts of things after you-if we set Alex free by Black Magic we could open up other voids. The tie between darkness and Alex will always exist and he will become haunted by those on the other side."

"So . . . like . . . how?" asked Charlie, sitting on the other side, still wearing his slightly bemused expression, head in his hands with a frown on his brow.

Anya sighed and sat down.

"It's used by-shall we say-the demons of this world; Red Caps, Mr X, Demons. They all use it for a bad purpose; that could be to put someone under a spell-make them do things they wouldn't normally."

Shea suddenly had a mental flash of Alex. Had he been under such a spell when he wished his parents dead? Thinking about it-what about Grace? Was *she* still under one? Shea glanced over at her. The pale child was sitting with her head thoughtfully in her hands. She shook her head and jerked herself back to the present.

"The problem is" she ventured "that we don't really know where Alex is. I mean, sure, we know he's in the void, but whereabouts? I don't reckon he'll have stayed on the edge, not with Mr X after his blood. He'll probably have gone into hiding. We don't even have the dagger."

Again, the flash of a mental image. Alex, hiding behind a large yellow rock with clouds in the distance. Shea blinked. Stupid mind. Overtired, probably.

Charlie looked puzzled.
"So-o . . . any other ways to get him out?" he asked.
Anya shook her head.
"None that I know of." she admitted. "I'd have to go back and look."
"So . . . what? We just sit around until we find something?"

Anya looked coolly across at him.
"Unless you have a plan . . . ?"

Charlie shook his head, looking dejected. He couldn't believe they didn't have a plan. They always had a plan-well, mostly. Not that his brain was really in the mood for thinking about it. He sighed and laid his head in his arms. No plan, no Alex. Couldn't they just let it be?

"Listen," Anya was saying "I know you're angry. We all miss him. If it wasn't for Alex, we'd most likely all be dead by now. But I don't think you can bring back dead people, which is what he technically is now he's in the Underworld. Even with black magic, it would have to be very powerful. And dangerous. Most likely there'd be a sacrifice."

Charlie grimaced. A sacrifice? Eugh!
"So is there no other way?" asked Shea. She didn't look like she wanted to give in.

Anya shook her head.

"No, Honey. I don't think there is."

She sat down and put an arm around her friend, who seemed like she was about to burst into tears.

"But . . . we can't just give up." Charlie protested. His mind reeled at the thought of not having Alex back. "We can't, we just, we just-"

Grace was looking thoughtful. She had the expression of a troubled mind written all over her face. As Charlie glanced across at her, she frowned, and shook her head.

"No, what?" asked Charlie. Grace looked up.

"I was just thinking." she replied. "Wasn't Alex like a, like a . . . wolf, when he, y'know, got sucked in?"

Anya nodded.

"Well, I was just thinking that . . ." Grace seemed to be having trouble expressing her thoughts. "Well, if he's like, not human, or whatever, shouldn't that mean he hasn't really died? Like, not a human death?"

Shea nodded. Anya however shook her head. "No, Alex was part human."

"Yeah, but he was also part demon, too." replied Charlie, grasping to the thin straws Grace seemed to have offered him, "When he went into the portal, I mean."

"Mr X . . . . well, he gets creatures out of the portal all the time." said Grace to the table. "He must have done. When I was there, there seemed to be more and more all the time. That's why he needed my blood. I mean, to open it. That's what he uses the dagger for. He has to get them from somewhere."

"Yeah, and I bet they can't multiply that fast."

Anya shot Charlie a dirty look. "Demons don't really die though, "she told them, forcefully. "They like . . . disappear."

"Oh yeah?" asked Charlie, raising his head off his arms, "Where to?"

"Oh, well, I mean, I don't exactly know where to . . . it's like . . . just . . . another place."

"Like where?"

"I don't know."

Charlie sat back in his seat. "Just how many of these worlds are there?" he asked.

"I don't know. There might be just one. Or more. It depends."

"On what?"

"On lots of things." Anya told him. "We don't know where all the portals are. That's why they have researchers, like me."

"So . . . you find these portals?"

"Kind of."

"Kind of?"

"We have to look for a lot of things. They're not always portals. Sometimes it's like an energy rift, sometimes it's a cave, sometimes it's a hole. It depends. Sometimes we spend ages looking for something, and it never appears. There are known sites, of course, like Stonehenge-there's one near there, but we have to keep looking."

"And can these portals be re-opened?" asked Charlie.

"Sometimes. Sometimes they open by themselves. The one at Stonehenge opens about every hundred years. Others can be opened by force, like with Mr X-"

"Does he even have a name?" asked Charlie.

"-but others just, open."

"What, just like that?"

"Pretty much."

"Then what happens?"

"Well, either things come out or things go in. We've had a couple of disappearances. Demons have to feed, you see."

Everyone round the table pulled a face.

"And you . . . what?" asked Charlie

"Well, then someone has to close it, or make up a story, or convince anyone who's seen it that they're delirious. If things get out, they have to be tracked down *pretty* fast and destroyed."

"Sounds like a war."

"It can be."

There was a silence. Everyone seemed to be thinking.

"Look," said Anya, eventually, "there's nothing we can do at the moment. For all I know, Alex is dead, and that's that. To be honest, no-one I know who's ever gone through has come back again. I can search around a bit, but I'm not promising anything."

The crew looked up, grateful.

"Well, don't expect too much." warned Anya. "Thing is, all my books are at home, or in the research library."

"How you gon' get back?" asked Charlie.

"Well, not the way I came in-it took far too long. No, I think I'll fly back to London. They're probably wondering what on earth I'm up to. We've been gone for two months, do you realise? Two months without a report! James'll be so mad! No: there's nothing we can do. Let's just exchange numbers. As soon as I get home, I'll call: let you know everything that's going on. These last two months have really opened up a world for me-"

"And me." agreed Shea, pulling herself together "I've learnt so much. You're really interesting, Anya, you know?"

"Thanks. Well, if the tracker still reads straight, I think there's a station round here somewhere. I'll go from Glasgow. At any rate, I can't stay here; I've been gone God knows how long and they'll want a report on what I've been up to. Guess I'll have to figure my way around it. Tell them that I'm doing research."

Shea nodded. "How will we contact you?" she asked.

"Good point." Anya reached down in her bag. "This," she pulled it out, "was my cell. It's broken, as you can see. But I can get a new one with the same number. Here it is."

She pulled a piece of spare paper towards her, and wrote down the number.

"Zero, oh, three, one, two, four, seven, seven, three, eight, nine. There."

She wrote the new number three times, and split it between them, before both Charlie and Shea did the same. Grace took the numbers idly, unsure of what to do. Charlie winked at her.

"Don't worry," he told her "You'll be sticking round mine. You can call them numbers anytime you like."

Shea was tucking the paper into her top pocket: really it was the only safe place she had left.

"How long will it take you to get a new cell?"

"A day. Two, perhaps. Then they do all this security do-dah, but only if I tell them I've got a new one. Stops us becoming the hunted, see."

Shea nodded. "Right. Well, when do you plan to go by?"

Anya looked guilty. "Err, end of the week at most. Actually, the sooner the better: probably tomorrow."

"Right."

Everyone felt suddenly glum again. It felt like losing another team member. Despite their differences, Charlie was surprised by how close he suddenly felt to them all, and at how sorry he was to let Anya go. Without reason, it felt as though he'd known them, much more than just two months.

"Come on." said Shea, getting up. "We'll never find anything out this way. We'll just have to get on and do what we do, soon as possible. You'll go back, and let us know-soon as possible, you hear?"

Anya nodded.

"In the meantime, I guess there's no good in moping. We'll have to do something to cheer ourselves up-I mean we've got so far and we tried hard. And we certainly wouldn't be here without Grace. We still need to celebrate. So I say, who's up for a hot chocolate?"

THE END

THE NEXT DAY, Charlie was sad to wave Anya off. Shea had decided to let Grace stay with her a little while, suggesting she might prefer a more feminine touch before moving onto Charlie's. Charlie couldn't say he disagreed-in any case, it would give him time to clean up for the girl, considering the ordeal she'd been through, and the fact that she had no-where else to go.

He wondered just how long he could stay with Shea. It would be nice just to oversee Grace, even if it was only to make sure she was putting on weight. From personal experience he knew the things that could happen-he himself had crash-dieted only seven years ago, still suffering from the mental strains of that tragic New York happening. After all he'd been through, both there and here, he'd felt all the feelings a thousand times over-of worthlessness, of anger, of fear. From his guess, he couldn't stay long-one more person would be an extra burden, never mind two. No, he'd have to go home. Home sweet home. It would be good to be back, kind of. As long as Shea kept in touch, he'd be alright.

Actually, Charlie wondered what he was going to do, now that everyone was going their separate ways. He could carry on stealing, but somehow that didn't seem so dignified any more, and he didn't really want a new partner. Not that they would care that Alex was gone. Charlie looked around. He had to do it now; make sure now, if he was giving up, that he didn't take anything with him. As far as he was aware, he hadn't. Still, it might be safe to cover his back. Just in case.

And so they all went off. Charlie went home that Friday, seeing as he lived so close in town, adamant he was going to do *something*, though still not entirely sure what. At least they'd promised to try to get Alex back, and right now that was the most important thing on his mind. All the time they'd wasted doing nothing! And for what good? He'd lost his friend. But he could get him back; if he tried. There had to be another way to retrieve the dagger; Alex was still there somewhere, in the Underworld. No, he'd start the research. He'd find something. He was not giving up that easily. Charlie almost took himself by surprise; he had never realised what a big part of his life Alex had been. Without him it would seem desolate, and lonely.

That Saturday, Grace and Shea also came to the station to wave Anya off. Grace appeared to be fine, though Charlie was convinced she was secretly a little sad inside. Already she seemed alot less pale, and had put on some decent weight since getting back to civilisation. Still, it was only when the train left the station for London that Charlie truly realised how lucky he was to finally be back.

And so the journey ended, and our heroes separated-all but one. Grace stayed with Shea, who explained everything Anya had told her. Charlie took to the library every morning and night, searching, hoping for something that would give him a lead. Anya went back to her office and received a grand scolding from her editor in charge, who seemed furious she had not written in two months, and refused to give him a whole account of what she'd been up to. Still, that didn't stop her catching up, producing a wonderful story about life in remote Scottish towns that earned her the front page. And, yet, all the while, she always seemed to be looking. Always researching just odd little things, things that neither her manager, nor the rest of the team could understand. And then there was that strange little book she carried with her . . .

THREE MONTHS
LATER

"Got it!"

Creative writing Productions

Founded: 2008

Members:

Samantha Bill (Y11)
Philippa Wheatley (Y11)
Nicholas Vaughan (Y11)

Rebekah Jones (Y10)
Benjamin Watkins (Y10)
Toby Collier (Y10)

Follow us on Facebook: James Bookie